BEEF CAKE

FIGHTING FOR LOVE BOOK #2

JIFFY KATE

WWW.SMARTYPANTSROMANCE.COM

COPYRIGHT

PROLOGUE

FRANKIE

Two Years Ago

They say curiosity killed the cat.

I'm the cat in this scenario, but I'm hoping I don't die. That would really suck.

As I step out of my car in a dark parking lot of the Dragon Biker Bar in the outskirts of Green Valley, Tennessee, I seriously begin to question my sanity.

What am I doing?

Sure, I want answers. But I'm also pretty sure there's a way to do that in the daylight and somewhere safer. However, my work hours keep me tied to Maryville Hospital and when I'm not working a shift, I'm sleeping. That's how it is when you're fresh out of college, putting in nursing hours in the ER, working on your physician assistant training, with no seniority—you get shitty hours and all the shit no one else wants or likes to do. Just a lot of shit. I remind myself it won't always be like this and I love it. Call me crazy, but I actually love taking the difficult patients and doing the things no one else wants to do.

I'm always up for a challenge, which also might explain why I'm here.

At this shady looking bar with a parking lot full of bikes.

This is the hangout for the notorious motorcycle club, the Iron Wraiths.

Up until a week ago, I didn't know who they were. I'd never heard of them. I haven't lived in Green Valley long, and like I said, when I'm here, I'm usually sleeping. So, after an awkward encounter with a few of them at the gas station, I mentioned it to my mother on my weekly visit.

Her reaction is why I'm here tonight.

Over the years, she's been so subdued about... well, everything. If I ask about our past or my father, she nonchalantly passes over it, stating we're better off without him and that my childhood was uneventful.

But there's something inside me that's always revolted against that. *Lies*, that's what my gut says. The nurse in me wants to get to the bottom of it—of my life.

When I go to grab the handle of the front door, it flies open and a man the size of a house runs out, nearly knocking me over. Glancing behind him at the inside of the bar, it's utter chaos—overturned tables, shattered beer bottles, a few broken chairs, and people everywhere.

There are a few women huddled together in the corner, just inside the door, and clusters of men on the floor. And blood... lots of blood.

I want to run.

I hate violence.

But I can't.

My need to help won't allow me.

People are suffering and I can help.

Walking blindly into the dark bar, I kneel down beside the first group of men I come to. "I'm a nurse," I inform, to which I'm greeted with harsh, confused looks. "Let me help him."

It's obvious the man has a severe wound to his stomach. The blood soaking into this shirt tells me it's probably a stab wound, but

2

not too large or too deep. Thanks to my physician assistant training, I'm skilled in suturing wounds and giving stitches.

Eventually, the two men flanking him move aside and let me get closer. Pulling back the man's bloodied hand, I see the laceration is small, maybe an inch or so, just the right size for a blade to enter and exit cleanly. He's not coughing up blood, just in pain, so I go through a series of questions I'd ask if I were in the ER.

What's your name?

Can you tell me what happened?

What level is your pain?

Most of the questions are answered with a grunt, so instead of depending on my patient to give me details, I get to work.

"I have an emergency bag in my car," I tell the man to my right. "It's a Mustang…" I stop myself. "The only car in the parking lot. The bag is grey and it's in the backseat."

Without waiting for a confirmation or any sort of agreement, I reach the hem of the guy's t-shirt and rip.

"That's hot."

Turning sharply to my left, I see the other man hovering over me, watching my every move, but it's not because I'm tending to his friend. It's more sinister than that. He's somehow turned on by my ministrations and it pisses me the fuck off.

"Go find some towels," I demand, not letting him get to me.

I'm good at this—blocking people out, focusing on the task at hand. It's what I do. It's where I feel most like myself and at ease. Somewhere in the face of trauma and chaos, I find peace.

After I patch the first guy up, another meaty motorcyclist comes and grabs my arm, forcing me over to a make-shift hospital bed where another older guy lies, writhing in pain, holding his shoulder.

"Can I take a look?" I ask, grabbing his attention, probably because outside of the few women I saw when I came in, I'm the only female around. Actually, I lost track of those women and I very well could be the only woman in the bar. That should probably bring me pause and make me run, but I'm in the trenches now. This dingy, roadside bar has become my ER. I won't leave until I'm sure everyone survives.

Doesn't really matter if they're in-laws or outlaws.

I'm not a doctor. I haven't taken the Hippocratic Oath. But I have pledged my life to saving people. And something tells me I was meant to be here. Why else would a woman who steers clear of any sort of violence walk into a bar just after a fight?

The universe wanted me here, so I'm staying until the last wound is stitched and then I'll make sense of the rest.

"Grab my bag," I tell the man who's been shadowing me ever since he retrieved my supplies from the car. "I'll need the alcohol and the gauze."

This cut isn't deep, in a spot that will make this old man wish he'd stayed home tonight.

"It'll probably be sore for a while," I tell him, reaching for the proffered alcohol. "And this is going to sting a little."

Do I get pleasure from making grown men cry? No. But it is slightly satisfying when I know they brought the pain on themselves. I'm not sardonic, but I believe in karma.

Half an hour later when everyone with visible wounds has been attended to, I gather up what's left of my supplies and start to tuck them away into my bag as neatly as possible. Everything will need to be sterilized or possibly even discarded, but I'll deal with that later.

Right now, the only thing I can think about is getting the hell out of here. And a hot shower.

"Not so fast," one of the men from earlier croons as he saddles up beside me, placing his large hand over mine. "The boys would like a word with you."

Boys?

I glance behind me, looking around, and definitely don't see any *boys*. I see men—some burly, others lankier, but all of them are wearing leather vests and exude an air of danger.

Someone turns on the lights and then everything somehow looks less and more scary all at the same time. Less so because there aren't any dark corners to hide in and I can see every face. But that's probably what makes it more so.

I can see *every* face.

Every set of eyes.

And they're all on me.

They're menacing.

Some sneering.

Some lingering.

All questioning.

"Who are you?" The man asking the question is standing at the bar, leaning against it like he's holding it up, or maybe it's holding him up. His eyes are squinted and his drawl is thick, but I can't tell if it's due to alcohol or just the way he talks. If I had to guess by the smell permeating this place, I'd opt for the former.

"I, uh . . ." I begin, faltering a bit as I brush my hair back and shoulder my bag, somehow feeling protected by its weight against my back. Also, hoping it's a stark reminder that I just helped a few of his men who would've been a lot worse off if I hadn't shown up. With that bit of information flowing through my veins, I straighten and start again. "I'm Frankie Reeves."

There's a flicker of recognition in his eyes, the exact response I was hoping for an hour ago when I drove my car into the parking lot.

This is what I wanted: to walk in here, go up to someone, tell them my name and get a reaction.

"Do you know my father?"

When the question is out of my mouth, the room around me fades into silence.

CHAPTER 1

GUNNAR

"*Oh, yeah, that's it!*"

You know when you're somewhere between dreaming and waking up and you're unsure what's real or not?

That's where I am right now.

"Right here," he says, somewhat out of breath. "That's perfect, baby. Stay still, though, I don't want to hurt you."

"Don't worry about me, I can handle it."

I could've sworn I was having a sex dream but now, I'm not so sure.

Bang, bang, bang.

They're going to break the fucking bed with the way the walls are shaking.

"Shit, it's still not going in all the way. Do it harder, Cage."

And, I'm awake.

Hearing my oldest brother's name being called out and told to *do it harder* is enough to kick me out of the deepest sleep.

Guaranteed.

Bang, bang, bang.

"That's it! Just a little more, babe. You've almost got it."

"I don't want to break it," Cage growls out in frustration.

"One more stroke and you're there."

My god. There aren't enough pillows in the state of Tennessee to bury my head in to block out the sound of my brother and his girl-friend having sex.

Also, is he trying to kill the poor girl? He's twice her size and it sounds like he's trying to plow her through the damn wall.

BANG.

"That's it!" she exclaims, elation thick in her tone. "You did it!"

"I couldn't have done it without you, babe." He sounds out of breath and it's all I can do to keep last night's dinner from spewing all over the bedroom. I could've lived *another* twenty-two years without being witness to this exhibition.

"That stud was a nightmare to get the nail through."

Huh?

"That's why these old buildings are so great," she says. "They were built to last, strong and sturdy, just like my Viking man."

Tempest's voice just dropped.

Why did her voice drop?

Cage laughs, and his voice is deeper and . . . husky? And that's my cue to get up and make it known I can hear everything going on before things *really* get going. It also might be time to move to the other side of the apartment.

Or the fucking state.

I've been here in Green Valley for a week and it's been great so far, but I don't want to cramp their style or make things uncomfort-able. I also don't want to inadvertently be a third wheel to their fuck-fest on a regular basis.

That happened too many times back home with my other brothers and it's a trend I don't care to continue. If I had a job, I could move into my own place, but Cage is a fucking hardass and the training schedule has been brutal. Any employment outside of training for a fight and teaching classes is out of the question. But I wouldn't have it any other way. That's why I'm here—to train and be the best, and eventually, to be as good as him.

By the time I've dressed, brushed my teeth, and opened my door,

8

Cage has Tempest pushed up against the wall across from my room with his tongue down her throat, right next to the framed picture they obviously just hung.

Tempest immediately pulls away and hides her face in his chest as she chuckles, but my brother can't bother to even pretend to be embarrassed.

"Just let me get to the kitchen before you two attack each other again, please," I mutter, quickly walking past them, avoiding all eye contact.

Tempest calls out, "Sorry!" But Cage follows up with, "No, we're not," before I hear a door slam closed.

Quickly, I fix myself a protein shake and head downstairs to the studio to begin my morning workout. I'm not mad at the lovebirds upstairs, not in the least. I'm thrilled Cage has finally found his person and is in love. But I've just met Tempest and, although I think she's great and perfect for my brother, I'm not comfortable seeing her being manhandled by the guy.

I'm used to my brothers bringing random chicks to the studio and to the house we used to share, but I knew I'd most likely never see the women a second time. In this case, I'm pretty sure Tempest will become my sister-in-law, sooner rather than later, and I'd rather not know any intimate details about her, if you know what I mean.

My warm-up takes the usual thirty minutes or so and then I switch to my official workout. It's seamless, one flowing into the other. It's like breathing to me: easy but necessary. I need to feel the burn of my muscles, the sweat rolling down my body, the tightening of my lungs every day. It helps to clear my mind and stay focused while getting me closer to my goal of being the top MMA fighter in my weight class.

I've been going at it for a good hour when Cage finally waltzes in, his smile making it very clear he was *going at it good* too, but in a different way.

Asshole.

Between punches, I glance at him, giving him an intense glare just like I would an opponent. I swear if I wasn't wearing boxing gloves, I'd flip him off just for being his smug self and silently rubbing his sexcapades in my face. It's been way too long since I've been balls deep in anything besides my palm and I don't appreciate being woken up with a resounding reminder that, once again, Cage gets everything he wants.

And he's the best at it.

Fucker.

He's even good at retiring, even though it was forced upon him thanks to a career-ending injury. Regardless, he's excelling at it, totally making it his bitch. This new gym is everything he ever wanted Erickson's to be and more. It's personal, one-on-one coaching. There isn't any showboating. Everyone is treated equally.

Sure, he doesn't have many patrons yet, but he's building a good, solid foundation. Besides, once I go pro, he'll have all the publicity he can handle, and I'll be doing for him what he spent his career doing for our family gym back home.

"I'm sorry, man," he finally says, breaking the silence with a laugh. When he sees I don't believe his bullshit, he holds up his hands in surrender. "I am, I mean it."

Eventually, I hold my punches and face him straight on. "Look, I'm happy for you and Tempest, but I really don't want to walk in on the two of you fucking. If I need to find another place to live, I will."

"Don't be stupid, G. We've had this place to ourselves for months; you've been here a week. It's an adjustment for all of us, but we'll make it work."

A few beats pass before I give him a nod, sweat dripping off my hair and onto my forehead. After swiping the back of my covered hand over the damp skin, I continue hitting the bag in front of me. I know he's right, and I'm damn thankful to be here. Without Cage and this opportunity, I'd have to tuck tail and go back to Dallas and get lost in the mix of Erickson MMA. With all the big names and bigger egos, that's the last thing I want.

Even though Green Valley, Tennessee is a culture shock, it's already growing on me and it's the perfect place to buckle down and focus on my end-goal—be the best, no distractions, make it to the top.

I'm toweling off an hour later when I hear Cage call my name.

"Yeah?" I holler back.

"Can you give me a hand hanging this new bag?" he yells from the other side of the studio.

Recently, he acquired another portion of the strip of old buildings the studio resides in. It's a great set-up. He and Tempest have turned the upstairs into great living quarters, and everything below is nothing but mats and bags with mirrors lining most of the walls. Eventually, Cage plans to build a ring in the middle of the new building, amping up his arsenal of training equipment.

Fuck, before he's done, this place will be better equipped than Erickson's. He'll have enough space to host his own events. Being in the backwoods of Tennessee, there's nothing like this for miles. You'd have to go into Knoxville to find something even close, but all of those gyms lack one thing.

Cage Erickson.

I might be biased seeing as how he's my older brother and I've always looked up to him, putting him on a pedestal, but it's true. Before his injury, he dominated the sport. Everyone wanted a piece of him even though they knew they couldn't beat him. They just wanted the bragging rights: *I fought Cage Erickson—The Fighting Viking.*

I want that.

I want to be everything he was . . . but better. I'm going to fight smarter and be in it for the long haul. It's all I've ever wanted. Now that I've paid my penance and finished college—something Cage never did—I'm going for my real goals.

"On my way," I finally call back, tossing my towel down and jogging over to where he's standing on a tall ladder, marking where to drill bolts into a beam that's attached to the ceiling.

"Hold the ladder," he instructs when I walk in. "This thing is shaky as fuck and if I don't get this in, I'm going to Hulk smash this place." He mutters continuously as he positions the bolt and begins to drill.

Hanging bags is something my brothers and I have done together for years and we usually make quick work of it. This time, though, is proving to be more difficult.

Cage has managed to strip a couple of bolts trying to drill them into the old steel beam and he's getting more pissed by the second.

Meanwhile, I'm trying not to laugh and piss him off even more.

"You got a good grip on the bag?" he asks when he finally gets the bolt in and attaches the hook.

"Got it," I tell him, ready to get this shit over with so we can go back to training.

As I'm holding the bag, I feel the tension give way. Instinctively, I look up just in time to see the chain whip through the air.

I try to drop the bag and guard my face, but I'm not fast enough. The impact of the chain hitting my face knocks me off balance and I fall to the floor with a thud.

"Oh, shit, man! Are you okay?" I hear Cage jump down off the ladder and the next second he's kneeling down beside me, hovering. "Let me look at your face."

"I'm all right, just a little stunned." I hiss, pressing my hand to the skin and feeling a sting. "I might have a shiner, but those are a dime a dozen around here." Sitting up slowly, I try to get my bearings.

Cage curses under his breath before rushing off. Seconds later, he tosses a towel at me with instructions to hold it to my cheek then grabs his phone and calls Tempest.

"Hey, baby. Look, we've had a bit of an accident in the studio and I have to take Gunnar to the ER." His eyes grow concerned and he draws his brows together when I bring the towel away from my face and we both see all the blood. "No, I'm sure he'll be fine, but I'd rather a professional check him out just to be safe."

My stomach rolls as I register how the once-white towel is now bright fucking red. You'd think being a fighter, I would be good with blood, but this is more than I'm used to. Besides that, typically when

I see blood, it's usually coming from someone else. Not to be overly cocky, but I'm a damn good fighter.

"Keep that towel on your face, dammit," Cage orders.

"Where the fuck is it coming from?"

Come to think of it, my face feels a little numb.

Cage grabs me by the arm and helps me stand, then quickly guides me outside to his truck.

Once I'm seated and buckled in, he jumps behind the wheel and takes off, tires screeching as we leave.

"You have to talk to me, man. What's going on?" I'm practically begging for answers because all I know is my face is bleeding and we're headed to a hospital somewhere. My brother's silence, while probably soothing for him, is only causing more panic to rise in me.

"I think the chain that hit you must've had a jagged edge because it sliced the shit out of your cheek. I'm sorry, man . . . that's on me."

Hearing the worry in his voice is concerning.

I've always looked up to Cage, idolized him probably more than I should, but he's always taken care of me. I can see it all over his face that he feels like he's failed me somehow because of a stupid accident that could've happened to anyone.

"Shit, bro. I know you hate me being better looking than you, but you didn't have to fuck my face up," I say, trying to diffuse the tension with some humor. When he takes his eyes off the road for a second to look at me, I give him a wink and the best grin I can manage, but he doesn't take the bait.

"It's not funny, G. You could've been seriously hurt. It could've sliced your fucking eye or something . . ."

I hear the unspoken truth. It could've sliced my eye and taken me out of the ring—and ended my career before it ever got started. But it didn't.

"It's just a flesh wound," I joke, quoting our favorite Monty Python movie. This gets a smirk out of him and I see his shoulders relax some.

"Where the hell is this hospital you're taking me to?" I ask as

Green Valley fades into the rearview mirror and nothing but trees frame the road.

"The closest hospital is in Maryville, about thirty minutes away." He glances over once more, giving me a furtive stare. "Keep that towel pressed on your face . . . we don't need you losing too much blood."

I can't help the laugh that escapes me, but I quickly shut that shit down. The splitting pain from my face moving is enough to make my stomach roll again. The initial numbness I was feeling is fading and now, I have to admit, I'm kind of nervous.

Put me in the ring with someone twice my size and I'm good.

Stick me with a needle and I'm the biggest pussy you've ever seen.

"Think I'm gonna need stitches?" I ask, sounding more like a kid than I've felt in years.

Cage sighs, his right hand leaving the steering wheel and settling on my shoulder, giving it a squeeze. "You're going to be fine."

Just like always, I believe what Cage tells me—because in all my twenty-two years, he's never steered me wrong. For my entire existence, he's always been there to back me up and right my wrongs. When our other brothers would give me shit as a kid, Cage would come to my defense.

Maybe it's our difference in age? Him being seven years older than me might've put enough years between us that I didn't annoy the shit out of him like I did Viggo, Vali, and Ozzi. Or maybe it's our similarities? When I say I've always looked up to Cage, I mean it. It's been from day one.

My first memory of him is in a ring. I was probably four and we were watching one of his early fights. It was in a dingy, rundown gym and the kid he was fighting was taller and bigger, but my big brother didn't let that scare him. He fought that giant with everything in him, leaving it all on the mat.

I remember the roar of the small crowd when everyone cheered for him. It was the first time I *knew*, without a shadow of a doubt, he was awesome and I wanted to be just like him.

When we pull up at the hospital, Cage parks the truck in front of the emergency room. Walking inside, I see the lady at the window and watch as her eyes go wide at our approach. I'm pretty sure it has nothing to do with my injury and everything to do with the beast at my side. Plus, I'm no small cookie.

Together, we probably look very menacing. If you didn't know Cage, you'd probably think he's some kind of assassin. He's a scary looking mother fucker. I'm not as big as he is, but we're built the same and look a lot alike—same ice blue eyes, same blond hair.

"He's got a nasty cut," Cage offers. "We're going to need to see a doctor right away." His tone is direct, leaving no room for discussion.

Her eyes snap from Cage to me and then back to Cage. "Yes, sir . . ."

There's a buzzing sound and the doors to our left open and she meets us there. "Follow me. You can fill out the paperwork while you wait for the doctor."

Once we're in one of the curtained-off areas, I have a seat on the edge of the bed while Cage paces the small space, making it feel even smaller and making my anxiety spike.

"Sit the fuck down," I tell him once the lady leaves. "I told you, it's a flesh wound . . . I'm fine."

He stops, turning and running a hand down his face. "Sorry . . . I'm just thinking of what Mom's gonna say when she sees your face."

I roll my eyes. "Like she hasn't seen worse."

Our mother is married to a fighter and has raised five boys who all spend time in the ring, if not professionally, then recreationally. She's no stranger to injuries. Over the years, she's seen us all beaten to a bloody pulp. That can't be easy, which is why she's probably so strong—hardened, even. She can't help it. It's the only way to survive living with people who throw themselves in front of a punch for the love of a sport. Definitely not for the faint of heart.

Cage occupies himself with filling out the paperwork the lady brings back, which is helpful because the blood still hasn't stopped flowing from my face. I've had my fair share of split lips and cheeks over the years, but nothing that's bled quite this bad, which leads me to believe it's deeper than I thought.

After a few more minutes the lady from the front desk comes back and takes the paperwork and my insurance card and driver's license. "Someone will be in shortly to take a look at that." She winces when I pull the towel back. "Might want to keep that there until the nurse gets here."

As the minutes tick by, I feel Cage getting antsier and antsier.

"What the fuck is taking so long?" he growls, running a hand through his hair, which is way longer than it's ever been. So is the beard he's sporting nowadays. I've always been the only one who kept my hair longer. I like the way it looks and it's something that sets me apart from every other Erickson. In a family as large as mine, you've gotta work to find your niche.

The hair is mine.

The ladies love it.

"You *really* look like a fucking Viking now," I muse, lifting my legs up onto the bed and reclining back. If I'm going to be here a while, I might as well make myself comfortable.

Cage gives me a smirk. "You're just jealous of my manliness."

I laugh at that and then wince. "Shut the fuck up."

A few seconds later, the curtain pulls back and my heart stutters. Not from fear or anxiety, but from . . . attraction—pure, unadulterated attraction.

The woman standing at the foot of the bed staring at me has the most gorgeous brown eyes I've ever seen. They're dark and intense, standing out against her pale skin.

She's completely feminine without being overtly so. Her short hair gives her an edge I find alluring . . . I literally can't take my eyes off her.

"Mr. . . . uh, Erickson," she questions, eyes flitting from my brother to the chart and then up to me.

That's when the creamy skin of her cheeks turns a light shade of pink.

Clearing her throat, she immediately looks back down at the paper. "I . . . I'm . . ." She stumbles over her words for a brief second before she straightens her spine and clears her throat, obviously gaining full composure before looking back up at me. "I'm Frankie."

Her voice is a bit raspy and low for someone as small as she is. The majority of the population seems small in comparison to Cage, or even to me, but she's maybe a smidge over five feet and couldn't weigh more than a buck-twenty-five soaking wet.

"I'm Cage," my brother says, rising from his seat to shake her hand. "This is my brother Gunnar."

Apparently, I've forgotten my good manners and have been reduced to a heap of blood and bones, just staring at her, because Cage walks over and gives my leg a nudge.

"Uh, let me get you a gown. I'll be right back."

When she turns on her heel and pushes through the curtain, it flutters behind her in her haste. I look up at Cage, obviously appearing just as confused as I feel because he huffs out an incredulous laugh and runs a hand through his hair. "For fuck's sake," he mutters.

"What?"

"Nothing."

But it's obviously not *nothing* because he continues to smirk, shaking his head.

"Did I say something?"

Barking out another laugh, he turns to me. "No, dipshit. You didn't say anything. Actually, I was wondering if perhaps the injury is worse than I thought and we should have your head examined." He leans over the bed, putting himself right in my line of sight. "What's my name? What day is it? How many fingers am I holding up?"

He flips me off and I swat it down.

"Here." Frankie is back with a hospital gown that she tosses into my lap. "Put that on and let's get a good look at what we're dealing with."

Glancing down to the gown I realize, for the first time, I'm not wearing a shirt.

So, that's why she blushed. Mentally I give myself a fist bump. I've worked damn hard on this eight pack I tote around and I'm not ashamed of it or any other part of my body, for that matter. And this chick has elicited more of a visceral reaction out of me than any girl has in a long time, if ever, so I'm glad to know I have an effect on her as well.

Smirking down at the flimsy piece of fabric, I pick it up and set it at the end of the bed as I pull myself into a sitting position and toss my legs off the edge, bringing my body closer to hers and getting my first up-close encounter with Frankie.

Her scent is a bit sterile, like this hospital, but there's also a hint of something citrusy under all of that. I'd love to go in for a closer inspection . . . right behind her ear, where her pulse point is—heart beating wildly, pumping blood to the surface—and inhale.

"Let's just get to work," I tell her with a wink, hoping my dick stays put and doesn't make this even more uncomfortable than it already is . . . for her, of course.

"Lie back," she snaps, her eyes darting up to mine. A new no-nonsense air floats around her, walls of steel firmly in place, as her gaze turns cold and aloof. "This is probably going to hurt."

Have I mentioned I'm a perfectionist? When I get something—or someone—in my sights, I can't stop until I reach the top.

Ace the test.

Make the grade.

Get the degree.

Graduate with honors.

Win all the rounds.

Be the best.

And in this case, get the girl.

CHAPTER 2

FRANKIE

I was having a perfectly normal day. A pedestrian who ran out in front of traffic and got hit by a vehicle turning into the gas station came in earlier with a broken femur. Then, there was a man who was out shooting—for target practice, thankfully—and a buckshot ricocheted back at him and caught him right under the eye. Two flu cases, even though it's early in the season, and an appendicitis attack rounded out my day.

Until him.

Gunnar Elias Erickson.

Twenty-Two.

Six-foot-three.

Two hundred and thirty pounds.

A fighter with the most piercing, translucent blue-green eyes I've ever seen.

Growling out my frustration, I try to shake away his memory as I scrub my hands in the sink, getting ready to take my break and find something to eat. When you work in an environment like this, there are no normal time schedules or meal titles, like breakfast, lunch, and dinner. I just call them what they are—sustenance. You eat when you get a chance. You sleep when you get a chance. You pee when you get a chance.

Sometimes, people even fuck when they get the chance.

Not me.

I'm not into relationships. They're too complicated and take up too much time. I've never been one to need a man to complete myself. I feel complete all on my own, thank you very much. However, that doesn't mean I don't appreciate the opposite sex.

One time, a fellow nurse asked if I'm *asexual*. I'm not. I notice. I lust. I just don't act on it; not because the desire isn't there, but because my discipline is greater than the desire. Maybe I owe that to my mother. She's always made it perfectly clear that men bring complications.

According to her, safety is found in solitude.

I'm not the recluse she is, but I do see the reasoning in her irrational thoughts.

"Who was that *beefcake*?" Marie asks, saddling up beside me at the sink. My hands are now missing the top layer of skin. I've been scrubbing for long past the prescribed time, lost in my thoughts, all thanks to the *beefcake*.

Marie says the term like an endearment.

I, on the other hand, decide it's my polite southern way of calling him what I really want to call him: cocky, arrogant . . . violent. As I stitched him up, small talk led us to what caused the injury, which led to what he does for a living—or rather, what he'd like to do for a living. He's training to be a fighter. I don't like people who fight.

Maybe that's the nurse in me, unable to understand anyone who'd want to counteract what *I* do for a living. I'm in the business of making people well; healing their wounds, not giving them.

I've never understood violence.

That's another thing I can credit to my mother. She's always drilled into me to steer clear of it. Not just turn the other cheek, but run. When I was little, we played a game where she'd tell me the bad men were there and I had to run to my room and hide under the bed, pulling the boxes in front of me so I was basically invisible.

"Out of sight, out of mind," she'd tell me.

"He was a patient," I deadpan, hoping to end the conversation, but I couldn't be so lucky.

"He was sexy as hell," she muses, in one of those airy, breathy voices that says I'd happily sacrifice myself at his altar.

"If you say so," I mumble, tossing my paper towel into the waste bin and making my way to the exit. Maybe I'm just hungry? A little food and everything will be right with my world again.

She laughs, catching up with me. "I'm not the only one who thought so. Did you see the way Lana and Jody were staring? I swear, I thought they were going to drop their teeth on the floor."

Yeah, I don't want to have this conversation, but now that she's following me to the cafeteria, I have zero exit strategy. Not unless I want to head to the lounge for a repeat of last night's dinner: stale crackers and a granola bar that's probably been in my locker since I claimed it two years ago. So, basically, my choices are starving or letting Marie make my ears bleed. Guess I'll be deaf soon. It was nice having my hearing for the last twenty-five years; I'll really miss it.

"Are you even listening to me?" she asks, checking me with her hip as we turn the corner.

"Yes, he's hot . . ." I nearly vomit on the word. "And you want to mount him . . . but you'll gladly wait your turn, because even sloppy seconds with him would be better than any of the first courses you've had in your life." Pausing, I wait with my hand on the door. "Did I forget anything?"

Her smile turns conspiratorial. "I see what's going on here." Clicking her tongue, she nods her head and walks past me. "That's fine. You saw him first. Does he have any brothers? Oh, wait—was that scary dude with him related? Now that I think about it, they do have the same eyes. I mean, have you ever seen anything like it? Mesmerizing."

You want to know what's mesmerizing, Marie? Your ability to speak without breathing. That's impressive.

I smile, hoping it's somewhere between *you took the words right out of my mouth* and *stop fucking talking before you give yourself an aneurysm.*

Her head—and from the sounds of it, her panties—would literally explode if she knew there isn't just one brother, but five. Yes, five *fighting Vikings.*

How wonderful.

"How are you always so unaffected?" Marie asks, grabbing a tray and making her way through the line. "Not just with men, but with everyone. I swear, someone could walk in here right now with their head hanging off their shoulders by a thread and you would calmly set your tray down, walk over to them, and start trying to patch them up."

I shrug, grabbing a salad, because unlike everyone else around here, I don't want to die of early-onset diabetes. You'd be surprised how unhealthy health professionals eat. It's alarming. "It's my job," I tell her, unsure how to explain the way I compartmentalize. I've done it for so long, I don't even know how to undo it. "I just see a problem and try to work through it. Everything is a process."

Marie looks at me like I'm the one who's lost her head. "If I didn't know better, I'd think you were a robot. But I've seen you bleed."

"Maybe it's synthetic," I tease, trying to redirect the topic.

That's enough of Francis Reeves 101, but Marie's not far from hitting the nail on the head: I don't get attached. That's the bottom line.

It makes me a great nurse, but a shitty friend.

CHAPTER 3

GUNNAR

"*H*ands nice and tight," Cage yells. "Relax your fucking shoulders."

I huff, sweat dripping onto my face. "They're as fucking relaxed as they can get," I yell back.

The next thing I know, I'm no longer facing my sparring partner, Vince, and Cage is in my face. "Don't talk to me like that when you're on my mat. My studio, my rules. My opinion is the only fucking opinion that matters. If I say you're breathing too much, you better slow that shit down. Understood?"

Nodding, I know what's coming next, but the past few weeks have been quite an adjustment. Going from brothers who can fight and get over it to a coach-student relationship is taking time.

"What?" Cage asks, his nostrils flaring.

"Yes, sir," I bark back, trying to tamper down my aggression.

"Again," he says, nice and even.

"Yes, sir," I reply, firm but without the attitude.

"Let's go again." He steps back and Vince resumes his position across from me, gloves up, and we begin.

Jab, jab, elbow, elbow.

Jab, jab, elbow, elbow.

"Nice stance," Cage calls out. "Front kick."

Jab, jab, kick.

Jab, jab, kick.

"Roundhouse, and then unleash," Cage coaches. My heart is now pounding in my chest, blood rushing through my ears, but this is the shit I live for. When most people would feel like laying down and dying, I'm just getting started.

Floyd Patterson had the Gazelle Punch.

Mayweather had the Shoulder Roll.

There's Pacquiao's Left Hand Straight and Tyson's Peek A Boo Defense.

And Gunnar Erickson's Gunman.

Don't look at me—I didn't title it, but it is my move. With my right arm extended, shoulders up by my ears, I snap my left fist out, making contact. Opponents have told me it's like being shot with a rifle, hence the name. Regardless, it's won me a shit ton of fights and it's my go-to move.

Of course, I'm sparing poor Vince the full brunt of the Gunman, but I still follow through with the move earning an enthusiastic *fuck yeah* from Cage as he paces the edge of the mat.

After we finish, the three of us are sitting around on the mats, shooting the shit, when Tempest walks down the stairs. When she sees us, her face immediately drops, turning stern. "What the hell?" she asks, throwing her hands out at her side and letting them slap back down loudly, getting our attention. "He still has stitches in his face and the nurse said no fighting for at least—"

"Seven to ten days," Cage finishes for her. "He's fine. It's been a week and they're starting to dissolve. Besides, he wasn't fighting. He was sparring." He jumps to his feet and approaches Tempest, closing in on her at the bottom of the stairs, his voice dropping.

"For fuck's sake," I mutter, rolling my eyes at Vince, who's only reaction is a smirk as he dips his head between his arms, avoiding eye contact.

Thankfully, Tempest swats the horn dog off and walks around him. "Well, in that case," she says hovering above me with a sweet smile, "how about one of you manly men run to the store for me so I can finish these double chocolate muffins I started."

When no one jumps at the chance, she adds, "There, of course, would be ample payment . . . in double chocolate muffins."

"I'll do it," I tell her, needing an excuse to get out of here for a few minutes. A drive to the Piggly Wiggly isn't exactly my definition of excitement, but since I haven't done anything except train for the last month, I'm an easy sell.

"Thank you," Tempest says, handing me a twenty. "I need a bag of dark chocolate chips and a bottle of Hershey's syrup."

My eyebrows shoot up in interest.

"Oh, yeah," she replies with a cocky grin. The Duchess of Muffins knows her muffins.

"Vince," Cage says quickly. "See yourself out." Swooping Tempest up and over his shoulder, she squeals before pounding on his back, demanding he put her down, but with zero force behind her fists or her words. "Gunnar, get lost on your way to the Piggly Wiggly . . . also, you should check out that pork-n-bean display on aisle six. Apparently, it'll just jump right out at you."

"Hey!" Tempest yells. "I knocked them down one time. And it was an accident."

"Can we not talk about pork-n-beans while you have my future sister-in-law thrown over your shoulder like a fucking caveman?" I ask with disgust.

That gets a laugh from everyone in the room, except me. I'm fucking serious about finding my own place.

A few minutes later, Vince and I make our way out of the studio, locking up on our way out as instructed, and I swear I can already hear the two love birds from all the way down here on the sidewalk. Surely there's some sort of sound ordinance that could be enforced.

I bet all it would take is one phone call to the police station, what with Tempest's rap sheet and all.

"Have a good night," I call out to Vince as he gets in his car.

"You too, man," he replies. "Gotta go home and ice my shoulder to get ready for Thursday."

I laugh, shaking my head as I climb in Cage's truck. Another thing I'm going to have to fix if I stay here much longer, besides getting my own place, is getting my own set of wheels.

Pulling into the parking lot of the small grocery store, I take note of the very few cars in the lot. I've always heard people talk about the sidewalks rolling up early in small towns, but I've never witnessed it for myself until now—and it's fucking true. The entire town shuts down when the sun starts to set.

With only two other cars in the lot, I park in front and don't even worry about locking the doors.

Small towns, man.

Who knows? It might grow on me.

The cashier greets me as I walk in the door and I have to smile. That would never happen in a big city. People run around like ants . . . or bees . . . whatever's busier. They don't pay attention to the person next to them, let alone a random guy walking into the grocery store . . . ten minutes before closing. *Shit.*

"Does nothing stay open late in this town?" I mutter to myself under my breath—or what I thought was under my breath, until a reply comes from the end of the baking aisle.

"Genie's. Woodie's, the Pink Pony . . . a couple of other bars, but that's about it."

I turn to the kid stocking the shelves and smirk. He doesn't even look old enough to know what a bar is and definitely not old enough to get into one without a fake ID. I had one once, but the need for it flew right out the window when I turned eighteen. Being tall and scary looking, thanks to my Scandinavian genes, has its benefits.

"Thanks, man," I tell him, tossing the bag of chocolate chips in the air and walking a few paces down, looking for the Hershey's syrup when a blur to my left catches my attention. That's when I smell her—the same citrusy scent mixed with the sterility of a hospital.

Glancing up, I feel my luck begin to shift. "Nurse Frankie," I muse, snatching a bottle of Hershey's from the shelf directly in front of her and earning a scowl. When her eyes meet mine, I expect a shift in demeanor but she schools her features.

"Your face looks good."

It's not a compliment, at least, not for me. She's complimenting herself on a job well done.

"The stitches are holding nicely . . ." she says, evaluating her handy work. "Shouldn't leave much of a scar."

"Just enough to give me some street cred," I tease. It's the same thing I told Cage when he kept going on and on about how bad he felt. If it hadn't been a rogue chain, it would've been a flying fist. I was bound to have a face wound at some point. So when it didn't come from the ring, that didn't discredit what it did for my face. "Admit it. I make this scar look good."

Frankie rolls her eyes and grabs her own bottle of Hershey's, tossing it in the shopping cart.

"Chocolate milk junkie?" I ask, wanting to make conversation with her. Maybe I could make a suggestion for putting that chocolate syrup to good use; I have a few ideas that all include the two of us naked.

What the fuck?

Shoot me. We're both attractive human beings. I'm attracted to her . . . my dick is attracted to her.

"It makes my spinach smoothie taste better," she deadpans, breezing past me.

Okay, so she's a health nut. That's cool. Me too.

"Have you tried powdered peanut butter?" I suggest. "Adds protein and tastes really good."

She stops her cart and turns to glare at me, but her eyes become hazy as they study my face, her lips parting softly. Goddamn, she's gorgeous.

For a moment, I think she's going to finally acknowledge this zing of electricity that's so obviously traveling between us. But instead, her stare shutters abruptly and she blinks, her jaw clenching tight. "I have five minutes before closing, five more aisles to make it through, and I've already exhausted all my bedside manner reserves for the day."

"I'm not your patient anymore, Frankie." I drop my voice, making her lashes flutter as I step closer. "You can be real with me."

After another prolonged hazy stare that has the base of my spine warming, a sharpness enters her gaze and she flicks her hand through the air dismissively. "I doubt very much someone like you is capable of handling my *realness,* Mr. Erickson." Her voice is a little breathless, and with that, she turns away.

Someone like you…

I can read between the lines, but it doesn't mean I like what I read. Someone like me? Fun fact about *someone like me*: The bigger the challenge, the more I enjoy it. Unbeknownst to her, she just made this—changing her mind about guys like me—my new favorite pastime.

"All right. How about we start with the basics. So, do you come here often?" I ask evenly, trailing behind as we both turn down the canned food aisle. I smirk at the display of pork-n-beans, thinking about what Cage said. Apparently, Tempest once had an encounter with this very display that sent the cans flying. The mental image makes me laugh.

"What's so funny?" Frankie snaps, and I realize she's stopped again in the middle of the aisle, her death stare aimed straight for my head. "Are you really so dense that you can't take a hint? Have all of those punches damaged your brain? Oh, wait. My bad. Y'all don't have brains to damage in the first place."

"Wow," I say, raising my eyebrows and the two items I came for. "Judgmental much?"

To that, she balks, her back straightening and her expression shifting from anger to indignance. She scoffs, tilting her head as she blinks her eyes, trying to find a rebuttal. But I don't let her. Instead, I decide it's time to correct some of her ignorant misconceptions about *someone like me.*

"For your information," I start, shifting both the chocolate chips and the syrup to one hand so I can point in her direction. "I graduated from college just like you. Yeah, I'm a fighter. I fucking love the sport, but that's what it is—a *sport*. I don't go out looking for back-yard or back-alley brawls. I'm not in a gang and I'm not a street-fighter. There are codes and discipline involved. I am an athlete."

Her expression finally softens, remorse shining from her eyes. "Sorry. I'm sorry. I just—I really don't like violence." I . . ." She takes a deep breath, and I get the sense saying these words is hard for her. "I don't like it at all. I'm sure you're a—"

"The store will be closing in three minutes. Please make your final selections and make your way to the front." A crackling voice comes over the store intercom system, interrupting her and this moment we're having.

Her eyes stay connected to mine for longer than a second and there's something in those chocolate browns that has the short hair on the back of my neck standing at attention.

I think we're having a moment.

"I have to go," she says, pink staining her cheeks. Before I can say anything, she quickly walks away.

And just like that, it's over.

I still want to know what she was going to say. I'm a what? *Nice guy?* She'd be right, I'm a really nice guy. *Fun guy?* Right again. *A great lay?* Ding, ding, ding. *Someone she should go on a date with?* Tell her what she's won, Johnny.

Instead of prodding, I make my way to the checkout and place my two items on the belt, giving the cashier a crooked smile. "Sorry for keeping you so late."

"Oh," she says with a blush and a smile. "I don't mind. Nothing else going on in this town."

"Right?" I say, digging my wallet out and grabbing the twenty Tempest gave me earlier.

"Besides," she continues, placing my two items in a bag, "Frankie is in here every Tuesday night, and always my last customer."

She takes the twenty and for a second I think she's going to stop there, but then she gives me a small smile with my change and continues, obviously desperate to make small talk. "She works at the hospital in Maryville and doesn't get back in town until late."

When I pocket the change and take the bag, the girl drops her voice and leans in, freely offering even more nuggets of information. "And between you and me, she doesn't get out much. Except for the farmer's market on Saturdays."

Farmer's market, huh?

Why am I not surprised about that?

Chuckling to myself—*small towns, man*—I give the cashier a smile and thank her just as Frankie walks up to the counter and starts placing her items on the belt. She made fast work, at least doubling what had been in her basket a few minutes ago. I don't look, but I can feel her eyes on me. I can sense her restlessness, like she wants to say something.

The cashier—*Katie*, according to her name tag—looks from me to Frankie and then back, obviously picking up on something between us. I decide to not make it awkward or cause Frankie any more grief for the night and give them both a short wave as I head out the door.

Some instinct has me waiting in the truck, and I watch Frankie carry her two sacks out to an older Mustang and start the engine. Once I'm satisfied she's safely in her car, I drive off, trying not to feel like a creeper—and failing miserably.

CHAPTER 4

FRANKIE

I woke up in a funk today, which is weird because Wednesdays are one of my favorite days. I blame my late-night encounter with Gunnar Erickson. After our run-in at the Piggly Wiggly, I thought he was going to follow me home and I was going to have to call the cops, but fortunately, he went his way and let me go mine. But that doesn't mean I didn't think about him.

No, that would be the furthest thing from the truth. I replayed our conversation, along with visuals, many times. Unlike the first time we met in my ER, he was wearing a shirt, but that didn't keep me from remembering what he looked like without one.

And that kept me up past my bedtime.

So, this funk is all his fault, which makes my dislike for him increase. He's messing up my sleep pattern, making me have inappropriate thoughts . . . and dreams. Yeah, he's even muscled his way into those too. And now, he's messing with one of my favorite days of the week. I volunteer at the women's shelter in Maryville on Wednesdays and Fridays and it's my happy place.

Some of my earliest memories are from the shelter. Most people's memories start sometime around their third or fourth birthday. Some earlier. Some later. I'm later—way later. I was seven and I vividly remember Helen, the director, giving me a small, brown stuffed bear. She also took me to their clothes closet and let me pick out an outfit. I chose a rainbow shirt.

Everything before that day is void.

I don't remember a birthday or Christmas. There's not a special day that sticks out, but there's no bad one, either. I've asked my mother for information, needing something to piece together the first seven years of my life, but she always shuts me down, telling me there's nothing good about our lives before we went to live at the shelter. She's glad I don't remember, and that makes my need to know that much more intense.

When she gives me half-truths, it's like she still sees me as a child—someone she can pacify with an altered version of reality. Now I'm not a child and I know her tells, but I no longer press her for information. After being denied for so many years, it seems like a waste of time. After college, I decided if I was ever going to know anything about my life before the age of seven, I would have to figure it out myself.

As I pull into the parking lot of Daisy's Nut House to grab a cup of coffee on my way out of town, the familiar roar of motorcycle engines behind me makes me pause. For a split second, I think about getting back into my car and forgetting the coffee, but then I straighten my spine and sure up my resolve.

I'm not scared of them.

They have no power over me, except what little I give them to make them think they do.

This is a free country and I can go anywhere I want and do whatever I please.

I can stop helping them at any time.

Those are my half-truths about the Iron Wraiths.

They're feared by many people in Green Valley and have a reputation of drugs, abuse, and debauchery. No upstanding citizen would seek them out intentionally. Except, I did.

My interaction with them is self-imposed.

I sought them out.

I did this.

I brought this on.

It's something I've had to remind myself over the past couple of years.

When I turn around, ready to face them and whatever favor they might be coming for today, I sigh in relief. The group of bikes pulling into the parking lot aren't the Wraiths. Their bikes are big and loud, but they're not wearing the leather cuts that now haunt my dreams.

"Morning," one of the men says as he swings his leg wide and dismounts his bike, holding it steady for the lady riding behind him to get off safely.

Nodding my head, I offer him a smile in return.

Yeah, *so* not the Iron Wraiths.

The entire group is made up of what looks to be middle-aged men and women, probably driving the scenic parkway on a leisurely bike ride. Like normal people.

My heart takes a few more seconds to catch up with reality before it finally settles back into my chest, resuming its normal, calm rhythm.

Quickly, I walk into Daisy's Nut House and walk up to the counter to place my order.

"Morning. What can I get for you?" a younger kid asks, pulling a pencil and pad from the apron he's wearing. I smile at his eagerness. We could use more work ethic like this; Daisy trains her employees right. I've seen her in here a time or two, but mostly she just sits in the back, overseeing the operation.

"A jelly-filled donut and coffee," I reply, handing over exact change. I guess you could say I'm a creature of habit, but I can't help that I know what I like. Actually, I have a box of the jelly-filled donuts at my house. Daisy's donuts are available in the stores, but nothing beats a fresh one. Besides, I didn't have time to make coffee, and I can't eat a jelly donut without coffee.

"Have a nice day," the kid says, handing me a sack and cup. He must be new because I haven't seen him in here before. I feel like I know everyone. Or, at least everyone who works on Wednesdays. Before taking it, I slip a tip into his jar, replying with a, "you too".

As I exit the diner, I keep my head down while walking to my car. It's not that I'm not a people person, per se; I'm around people all day, every day. I love helping people. I love caring people back to health, but outside of pleasantries like what just took place—an exchange of money and goods or services—I'm not one for small talk. Of course, I have to converse with people at work, but I'm not the one seeking out gossip or sharing personal information.

I don't have relationships with people, except my mother.

Maybe it's her fault.

She's a recluse.

I'm not.

I live in a small house in Green Valley, Tennessee, and work at the hospital in Maryville, about thirty minutes from here. Some may say my life is monotonous, but I take comfort in knowing what to expect from each day.

My job is spontaneous enough to keep me from getting bored, as is the women's shelter. I find balance in the simple things, like going to the Piggly Wiggly on Tuesday evenings and volunteering my time at the women's shelter every Wednesday and Friday. On Saturdays, I take the things my mother makes and sell them for her at the farmer's market. If for some reason I can't make it—I occasionally pull doubles on Saturdays for the nurses who have a family—I drop the goods off to Gracie May Hill and she sells them for me. Well, for my mother, because like I said, she's a recluse.

She lives on a small piece of property at the end of a dirt road not far from Bandit Lake. It's a cabin her parents left her when they died —a place she frequented as a child. Up until I started college, she was a functioning member of society. We jumped around from rundown shack to trailer house, occasionally snagging an apartment for cheap, but always on the move.

Until the day I enrolled in college in Knoxville.

Believe me, I'd rather live there, or Maryville to be closer to the hospital, but I chose Green Valley to be closer to her. If I didn't go out there once a week, she would never see another human being. And that's not healthy. The nurse in me won't allow it.

Taking the donut out of the bag, I wrap a napkin around it and back out of the parking lot, headed for Maryville. I savor the donut, only eating a bite every few miles, washing it down with hot coffee and letting it settle my soul as I enjoy the scenery.

It is a beautiful drive, and one I never tire of.

Half an hour later, I'm pulling up to what looks like a church but is now the Women's Shelter of Maryville. It used to be a church, but has since been repurposed. I say they're doing God's work, so in theory, it kind of still is. I know it was a sanctuary for my mother and me all those years ago, as it's been for many since.

Walking up to the side door, I drop my trash in the bin next to the sidewalk.

Once inside, I place my bag in my small office and make my way out to the main hall.

Helen is standing with her clipboard, all business-as-usual.

"Good morning," I greet, looking past her to the people waiting. "How many do we have this morning?"

"You're early," she replies, looking at me with her own version of a smile. Helen and I are so much alike, it's scary. If you didn't know better, you might think she's my mother. But unlike my mother, who still looks so young and has beautiful blonde, naturally wavy hair, Helen's is darker, kind of like mine, with hints of grey. She wears hers in a tight bun at the nape of her neck. Like I said, she's all business.

She runs a tight ship around here. Everyone knows a well-run ship requires a stern captain to keep everyone in line, and that she does.

"Aren't I always?" I muse, not fazed by her briskness.

Once we get started checking in the newcomers, Helen and I work like the well-oiled machine we are. She gets all the pertinent information and I start interviewing, checking them over briefly and basically putting them into categories: battered, not well, well. Those who come to us with visible injuries get first priority with me. I look them over and tend to what I can. If they need further attention, we set that up with the hospital, which I am the liaison for. Most are just a little bruised. Some need a bandage. Occasionally, I stitch a busted brow or cut.

Today, I end up with a mother and her daughter sitting in front of me. They're no different than many other people I've checked out—and over—during my years of volunteering. Then again, they are, because they're the exact age of me and my mother when we came here.

And something about them is giving me major flashbacks, but I try to clear my head.

"Hello," I say, turning my attention to the little girl, giving her what I hope is a warm, comforting smile. Her dark hair is a bit matted, but even under the grime and grit that covers her ivory skin, she's adorable. She's clinging to a tattered teddy bear.

She tilts her chin up, enough to make eye contact but doesn't hold it and looks back down at her stuffed friend, picking at its matted fur. "Hi." Her response is meek and timid.

"She's shy."

Shifting my focus to the mother, I give her an understanding smile. "That's okay. Aren't we all from time to time?" I ask, looking back at the little girl and wishing I could give her a hug, which is alarming. I never feel like giving anyone a hug, especially people I just met and in a setting like this.

My policy is I never get attached.

Attachment leads to feelings and feelings lead to heartbreak.

I don't know where that stems from, but it's an understanding buried so deep inside me I can't seem to shake it. But there's something about this little girl that draws me to her.

After I get the little girl, Allie, settled with another volunteer who's showing a few new kids the playground out back, I turn my attention back to her mother. Her obvious worry makes my heart ache. Again, that takes me back, and I let out a deep exhale, willing myself to do what I do best—compartmentalize.

"Can I take a look at that cut?" I ask, pointing to the broken skin above her left eyebrow. It doesn't look fresh, and is probably too late for stitches, but it definitely needs to be cleaned and bandaged. When she still doesn't look at me, I add, "She's going to be fine."

And I don't just mean right now.

I want to tell her that I was her little girl once and I might not be the most open, loving person, but I'm not a horrible person either. I'm smart, capable, educated. I help people and contribute to society. There are things about me I wish I could change, but until I know all of the facts about myself, I'm not sure if that will ever happen. It's hard to know how to fix something if you don't know what's broken, which is why, even after all these years, I still push to know the truth.

As ugly as it may be.

There's an inscription on the side of the building we're standing in, and it reads: the truth shall set you free. Sometimes, I'm not sure what I believe, but that simple quote has driven me for the last eighteen years.

Eventually, the mother, Lisa, follows me to the room we've designated for examinations. Fortunately today, she's my only patient.

"Have a seat," I tell her, trying to use my most soothing voice, knowing she's probably scared and lost. "Do you have any other injuries I need to know about?"

She shakes her head, her eyes filling with unshed tears. But I can see the hard set of her jaw, and I believe her. There's resolve there and a strength I'm not even sure she realizes she has, but it's there, struggling to the surface. If I had to guess, it's what got her and her little girl to this safe haven.

"You're safe now," I tell her. "Helen has top-notch security, cameras at every entrance, both inside and out. The staff's top priority is keeping everyone safe." Sometimes, all a newcomer needs are those bits of reassurance. No one is getting in here without going through Helen first, and she's a force to be reckoned with.

As I go to clean the wound above her eye, she doesn't flinch or wince and I wonder what other unseen scars lie beneath. *Does she have one like mine?*

After I'm finished, I lead her down the hall to the closet where we keep clothes and other personal items. It's basically a place for the women to shop. Helen doesn't like to assume what people will want; she gives them a choice. And sometimes, the women who come through here would never ask for anything, but when it feels more like a choice, they'll take it.

Lisa picks out a clean shirt for herself and a pair of underwear. Then she takes some pants and shirt for Allie, along with a clean set of socks, underwear, and pajamas. It's then I know I really like this woman. You can tell a lot about people by watching them. She could've chosen anything in this closet for herself, but she stuck to bare necessities. However, when it came to her daughter, there was no hesitation and she was thoughtful in every article she chose, obviously picking things she knew would bring a smile to Allie's face.

A good mother always puts her child's needs above her own.

"Let me show you to your room," I tell her after she gathers soap and shampoo and toothbrushes. "There are clean sheets and a set of towels. While you're here, it's your job to keep everything inside these four walls clean. There's a community laundry on the other side of the main hall. Meals are served at seven, noon, and six sharp. If you miss one for some reason, Helen has provisions in the pantry. You'll have to see her to get them, but don't hesitate."

I pause and see her standing in the doorway, staring at the stark walls.

"I know it's not much—" I start, but she cuts me off.

"It's more than enough," she says, her eyes finally meeting mine and a tear slipping down her cheek. "Thank you."

When her arms wrap around my shoulders, I stiffen at first, surprised by the gesture. She obviously needs this, so even though it's out of my comfort zone, I hug her back.

And maybe I get a little something in return.

CHAPTER 5

GUNNAR

I've been counting down the days until I can see Frankie again and it really pisses me off that tonight's sparring session ran long and I lost track of time. Even though I've tried to convince myself this is crazy and if we're meant to see each other again, it'll happen.

But then again, I'm just a guy going to the grocery store.

At nine o'clock on a Tuesday night.

And this is Green Valley. Like the overly talkative Katie the Cashier pointed out, if you don't want to go to a bar or out to eat by yourself, there really isn't anything else to do. At least not that I've found, yet, anyway.

I tried to make it by the farmer's market on Saturday, but Cage had me practically strapped to the mats the entire day. I swear, some days I feel like he's trying to kill me.

Last week, at this time, Frankie and I were going toe-to-toe in the middle of aisle six, and dammit if I wasn't hoping for a repeat.

I just need to see that spark in her eyes.

Gunning the engine, I fly down the quiet streets and hope all the on-duty police officers are preoccupied or sleeping on the job. If I do get pulled over, let's hope its Tempest's cousin, Cole. He's a cool dude. I met him for the first time last week. Cage has opened the studio up two nights a week to anyone in the police department to come and spar. It's a great workout, and a good way to promote self-defense while also keeping their skills on par.

In a town like this, where hand-to-hand combat isn't needed very often, it's easy to get complacent and rusty. So far, it's been a great success. Cage has even managed to get Sheriff James to stop by for a couple of workouts.

Slowing as I approach the grocery store, I'm hopeful when I see headlights. The closer I get, the more things come into focus—and I no longer like what I see.

Frankie's car is still out front, but it's surrounded by a few motor-cycles. Speeding up once more, I whip the truck into the spot beside Frankie and just as I'm climbing out, the bikes take off.

"Who were those guys?" I demand. I'm trying to reign in my concern and it's not working.

"Nobody," Frankie says, crossing her arms. There's always a protective air around her, like she's guarding herself against the world. "What are you doing here?"

"They look dangerous," I comment, ignoring her question because I want to know what she would be doing in a dark parking lot with them. Frankie doesn't seem like the kind of person who would keep company with bikers. She told me herself she doesn't like violence, and everything about those guys screamed violence.

Big bikes.

Leather vests.

Menacing.

I know, I'm one to talk. But there's a difference between those guys and their kind of menacing and mine. A huge difference.

And hey, at least I'm clean-cut and shaven. Well, I don't know about the clean-cut part. My mom would disagree. Out of all my brothers, I wear my hair the longest, but keep it pulled back in a low ponytail most of the time. And since arriving in Green Valley, I have let my facial hair grow a little. But my pretty face, as my brothers call it, keeps me from looking too scary. Cage on the other hand, not so much.

"You didn't answer my question," she says with a huff, turning to open her car door and making me scramble for an explanation so she won't leave.

I just got here, and I've been hoping all week to see her. I'm definitely not ready to watch her drive away again.

"I wanted to see you," I admit. There's no sense in beating around the bush. If she doesn't know I'm into her, then I really need to reevaluate my strategy, or up my game.

Opening the door, she turns her back to me and I see the way her shoulders lift then fall, and when she speaks, she sounds distracted. "Can you just—I can't deal with this. I don't have time to deal with you, okay? I'm not interested. Leave me alone."

I feel my entire body deflate. She wants me to leave her alone, I'll leave her alone. But since we're here, talking, and this might be my last chance, a part of me I can't ignore wants to make sure her disinterest isn't because I'm a fighter.

"Okay. Fine. But do you mind if I ask why?" I get the feeling she has her guard up all the time. I get it, I do. She's a beautiful woman, but it's got to be exhausting. Somehow, I'd still like to prove that it's not necessary with me.

She slowly turns back around. "Why what?" It's obvious she's trying to avoid answering, so I spell it out for her.

"Why aren't you interested?" I ask, keeping it casual and relaxed as I take a step back until my back is flush with the side of the truck. I don't want her to feel threatened or pressured, but I do want her to talk. So, I'm hoping if I give her a little space, she'll open up.

"You can be honest, it's cool." I shrug. "I'm just looking for some constructive feedback here. So, do you not find me attractive?" I ask, unable to keep from smiling. "Or are you just not into blondes? Or muscles?" I continue, trying a more playful approach, and it works. The side of her mouth pulls as she fights back a smile, her cheeks heating.

"I—you know I find you attractive," she mumbles reluctantly, the stain on her cheeks warming to red.

I nearly sigh in relief but stop myself, because this means her disinterest has its root in my fear. "Frankie," I continue softly, "is it because I'm a fighter?"

Her gaze cuts to mine and she presses her lips together, and that's all the answer I need. My stomach drops.

We stand there like that, watching each other, and she sways toward me, her eyes conflicted.

"Listen," I tell her, sighing, putting my hands in my pockets. "Go on one date with me, pretend I'm a lawyer, a doctor—"

She snorts, rolling her eyes. "I wouldn't go on a date with a doctor either."

"Fine, pretend I'm a window washer."

Now her lips twist to the side to hide a new smile.

"I promise I won't talk about MMA or cage fighting. Just one date. If you're still *not interested*, I'll leave you alone. And I'll leave you alone now if that's really what you want. All I'm asking for is a chance . . . and a date."

She eyes me and I can tell she's giving it some thought, which is hopeful.

Patiently, I wait for the final verdict, hoping it's not a no.

"You're incredibly persistent." Still struggling with her smile, she sighs in mock exasperation.

Am I proud of the fact I've convinced her to give me a shot in such a short time? Yes. And no. Yes, because I set out to do something and nothing makes me happier than accomplishing a goal. No, because I hate that I had to do it in the first place. I've never had to convince someone to talk to me or go out with me. But her misconceptions about me based on what I do don't sit right.

Thumbing my bottom lip, I give her a smirk. "I've been told my persistence is an attractive quality."

She finally—fucking finally—fully smiles, and it's everything. The sun, the moon, the stars. I swear it just lit up this dark-as-fuck parking lot. "Is that so?" Her tone is different. She's losing the chill and I'm thinking there might be a warm, soft center under that thick layer of ice.

And, fuck if I don't want to find out.

"Tomorrow morning," she announces, interrupting the fantasy of her curves under my hands.

Wait. What?

"Morning?" I ask, not sure I heard her correctly. With the blood leaving my brain and flowing to my dick, it's possible I wasn't paying attention.

Crossing her arms, she copies my stance, leaning against her car. "Yes, tomorrow morning. Daisy's Nut House. If we're doing this, we're doing it on my terms, and I'm busy. That's my only offer. Take it or leave it."

I get the feeling she thinks her *offer* is going to scare me off or change my mind, but she's badly mistaken. "Tomorrow morning," I confirm. "What time?" She could tell me two o'clock on the moon and I'd make that shit happen.

"Seven."

Again, the quirk of her head tells me it's a challenge. One I gladly accept.

"I'll be there at six thirty," I counter.

There's an air of skepticism whirling around, but I'll be happy to see her look of surprise when I'm sitting in the parking lot of Daisy's Nut House tomorrow morning when she arrives. Shit, I might drive over there now and sleep in the truck, just to make sure I'm early.

Her laugh, although disbelieving, is music to my ears. It might also be my new favorite sound.

Shaking her head, she gets into her car without another word and I stay put, watching her buckle up and drive off. I'm pretty sure she stops and looks back at me before turning out on the street. Could be my wishful thinking, but I'm going to roll with it.

I mean, she did agree to a date.

Fist pumping the air, I walk around the truck and get back in, starting it up. For a second, I let my mind wander back to what I drove up on—Frankie surrounded by those fucking bikers. I know I promised her I wouldn't bring it back up, but fuck if I'm leaving it alone.

There's one person I bet knows who those fuckers were.

I'll be paying my new friend, Cole Cassidy, a visit.

CHAPTER 6

FRANKIE

*W*hen I woke up this morning, I rolled out of bed like it was any other Wednesday. Walking to my closet, I pulled out a pair of jeans and a t-shirt. There's no need to dress up for my work at the shelter. I could wear scrubs if I wanted, but since I wear them almost every other day of the week, I take advantage of the opportunity to wear regular clothes.

It's when I'm standing in the mirror, trying to make my hair behave, that I remember what I agreed to last night.

A date . . . with Gunnar Erickson.

Six-foot-three.

Two hundred and thirty pounds.

And the most piercing, translucent blue-green eyes I've ever seen.

Gunnar Elias Erickson.

His question last night about me not being attracted to him is laughable. I'm so attracted to him it scares me. I've tried forgetting about him, wanting so badly to erase the memories of his chiseled chest out of my mind, but it's been futile.

Like it or not, he's apparently here to stay.

I also don't want to admit I was glad to see him last night. When he pulled into the parking lot, he unknowingly saved me from whatever favor the Iron Wraiths were after. They'd just cornered me in the parking lot a couple of minutes before and hadn't gotten around to saying what hoop they wanted me to jump through for the moment.

I've spent the better part of two years trying to prove my trustworthiness, and frankly, I'm getting tired of it. They're stringing me along and I'm desperate enough to fall for it.

When Gunnar drove up they took off, probably thinking they'd circle back around when he left, but he didn't leave. No, he was his typical, persistent self and I didn't hate it. Even though I tried to blow him off again, I really don't mind his company. He's surprisingly charming and nothing like I thought he'd be.

Sure, he's a bit cocky, but it's more endearing than annoying.

He's also not selling fake merchandise.

Everything he's packing is legit, which probably helps his case.

And slowly but surely, he's getting under my skin.

Part of me is hoping this morning's *date* is a bust and he proves my original judgment of him was right. Then I can walk away and not feel any regrets. But the other part of me, some dormant part I wasn't even sure existed, is hoping he proves me so, so wrong.

For a second, I think about adding a layer of mascara to my lashes or a swipe of gloss to my lips, but then I think better of it. Gunnar knows what he's getting. If he didn't like me the way I am, he would've given up a long time ago.

Unless, this is some kind of elaborate prank.

Yeah, there's that.

And it's totally plausible.

One time, back in junior high, Travis Evans pretended to like me for a few days only to humiliate me in front of the entire school when I tried to sit with him at lunch. It was mortifying and traumatizing and probably why I never attempted to get to know a guy again.

Ever.

It's not that no one has shown interest since then, but when I give them the cold shoulder, they give up. It's not hard to stay single when you have a thick layer of defense like I've built up over the years.

In high school, when I was ready to give up my virginity, I picked a guy I could tolerate—and who I knew wouldn't refuse me —and propositioned him.

The entire act was very clinical. I provided the condom and the perimeters—no calling afterward and no repeats.

It worked then, and it's worked every time since.

Not that it's happened much, but when it has happened, it's been the same arrangement.

When I say I don't do relationships, I mean it. I've never even been on a date. Which is probably why I'm suddenly nervous and thinking about standing Gunnar up.

A date.

I'm going on a date with Gunnar Erickson.

"It's a donut and coffee," I mutter to my reflection in the mirror. "You do this every day. The only difference is a beefcake will be sitting across the table from you." Groaning, I throw my head back and stare at the ceiling. Honestly, I'd rather scrub in on a surgery with Dr. Powell, and he threw a suture needle at me once because I set it up for a righty and it turns out he's a lefty. He's such an asshole, but at least I know what to expect with him.

I've never made the righty mistake again, that's for sure.

With Gunnar, every time he's around, I feel a flight of butterflies take off in my stomach . . . and my palms get sweaty . . . and my mind starts thinking inappropriate thoughts. It's unsettling, to say the least.

Tilting my head back up, I blink away the rush of blood and then pinch my cheeks. "Let's get this over with. Fifteen minutes, tops."

When I get in my car, I look at the time on my phone and it reads six forty-five, which is the same time I leave every Wednesday morning. The thought crosses my mind to call Helen and let her know I'm going to be there a little later than usual, but I decide to play it by ear. There's a chance I'll get there and he won't even show.

47

Or he will, but we won't have anything to talk about. Or I might chicken out and keep driving.

Yeah, there's always that.

But when I get close to the diner, it's not hard to spot the truck . . . and then the beefcake. He's leaning up against the side of the rusted metal—legs crossed, arms folded, looking like a dream. No, seriously, I had a dream just like this a few nights ago and I'm currently experiencing the strongest case of déjà vu I've ever had in my entire life.

What do they say about that?

Is it good?

Bad?

In another universe, someone like me and someone like Gunnar meet up for breakfast at Daisy's all the time? Have I crossed over some time-space continuum?

And this is a prime example of why Frankie Reeves can't have nice things. She screws it up with all of her overthinking and overanalyzing. And then she starts speaking about herself in the third person. It's embarrassing.

Get ahold of yourself.

I park my car beside Gunnar, and I don't miss the smile on his gorgeous face. With all the angular planes and hard lines, his soft smile is a nice contrast, setting off his mesmerizing eyes.

Oh, my God. I sound ridiculous, like one of those lovesick girls on the stupid dating shows the other nurses watch on our late night shifts. When he knocks on my window, I jump in my seat, my eyes flashing over to meet his, and he's holding a bouquet of flowers. Sunflowers, to be exact, which happen to be my favorite.

How did he know that?

What if he's a serial killer stalker?

That would be my luck.

"Hey," I say, getting out of my car and tamping down the rush of nerves.

He gives me an even bigger smile. Funny, I didn't think he'd be a morning person, but he's somehow just as chipper in the daylight as he is at night in the middle of the canned foods at the grocery store.

"Good morning," he muses. "Didn't think I'd be here, huh?"

I scrunch my nose and glance over at the door of Daisy's as another early riser walks in, letting the smell of freshly baked donuts waft out. "I don't know," I admit. *I was hoping you would . . . and I was hoping you wouldn't.* "But since you are, I guess we should go inside before the old men eat all the donuts."

"Have they run out before?" he asks, his expression going serious, like the idea of them running out of donuts is a tragedy. It really is. Daisy's donuts are hands-down the best in the state of Tennessee.

Letting out a laugh and appreciating the way the tightness in my chest eases, I shake my head. "Nah, I don't think so, but we want first dibs. They're best when they're fresh."

He nods his head in agreement. "True." Glancing down at the flowers that are still in his hand, he hesitates for a moment, shifting on his feet. It's possibly better than the flowers, because I realize then, he might also be a little nervous about this date. "I brought you flowers."

"Where did you get flowers at this time of morning?" I ask, taking them from him and holding them to my chest before turning and placing them on the passenger seat of my car.

"Tempest knows the florist downtown," he says, pinching his bottom lip like he's regretting his choices. "Is it too much?"

I thought I might see a different side of Gunnar this morning, but this is certainly not what I had in mind. He's surprising me again, but it's not bad.

"It's great," I assure him. Perfect, if I'm being honest, but I'm not ready to show all of my cards just yet.

As we walk into the diner, the same kid from yesterday is at the counter. When he sees Gunnar, his eyes widen and I have to fight back a chuckle. I wonder if Gunnar gets that everywhere he goes. If people reacted to me every time I walked into a room, I think I'd take a page from my mother's book and stay home. Attention like that makes my skin crawl.

"Good morning," he greets, schooling his features as he reaches for his notepad and pencil. "Jelly donut and coffee to go?"

I give him a smile, but then shake my head. "Two jelly donuts and two coffees . . . for here."

His eyebrows go up, surprised at this change of events.

"Can you add on a maple bar?" Gunnar asks, glancing in the case. "And a blueberry cake donut."

Turning around, I give him what must be a surprised expression because he laughs.

"What?" he asks incredulously. "I'm a growing boy."

The spit I was swallowing must have a bone in it because I choke and Gunnar pats my back until I can catch my breath.

"You okay?" he asks with a knowing grin, placing money down on the counter to pay for our breakfast. I would argue, but I'm still recovering, so I let him. It's just a donut and a cup of coffee. No big deal.

"Fine," I reply, as we make our way over to a table and have a seat, feeling a little hot. The air around us feels charged, but that's not new; it's been that way since the first day I met him in the ER. I've just been trying to ignore it, hoping it would go away. Like him, it hasn't.

"I thought you drink smoothies for breakfast?" The way he's leveling me with his eyes makes me fidgety. Now that I'm really getting an up close and personal experience with them, I decide they remind me of sea glass.

"Uh, I do. Drink smoothies. Every day, except for Wednesdays," I reply, still feeling mesmerized by the intensity of his eyes. I wasn't ready for those. The smirk? Sure. The biceps? Fine. The eyes? Nope. They turn me into a rambling idiot. "On Wednesdays, I eat jelly donuts."

The smile he gives me is a new one, different from all the rest. It's not his cocky smirk or his confident grin. It's a little wistful and a little mysterious . . . and a lot mine. I decide since I haven't seen it before now, I'm going to claim it. It's my favorite.

"Two jelly donuts, one maple bar, and one blueberry cake donut," the guy, who I now see has a name—Kyle—says as he sets down our donuts on the table between us. "I'll be right back with your coffees."

A second later, two piping hot cups of coffee appear and I smile up at him. "Thanks."

"You're welcome," he says, glancing over at Gunnar. "Is there anything else I can get you?"

"Looks great, man," Gunnar says, reaching for the maple donut. "Thanks."

I slide one of the jelly-filled donuts onto a napkin and take a bite. Strangely, it tastes even better than usual and I wonder if it's the fact I'm eating it while sitting down and not driving down the road. Or maybe it's the company.

"So, when you're not stitching up people in the ER," Gunnar starts, but pauses long enough to lick some icing off his thumb and drawing my attention to his mouth. "What do you do besides grocery trips to Piggly Wiggly on Tuesdays and getting donuts on Wednesdays?"

Taking a sip of my coffee, I try to decide if he's making fun of my simple life or just being conversational. "I also go to the farmer's market on Saturdays," I offer, gauging his reaction.

"That's right," he says, holding his half-eaten maple bar in midair. "Katie, the cashier at the Piggly Wiggly, told me that."

"Really?" I ask. "I didn't think she even knew my name."

Gunnar laughs. "Are you sure you're from here?" he asks. "Everyone in Green Valley knows everything about, well, everyone."

"I'm not really from Green Valley," I tell him, before I even have a chance to think better of it. "My mother and I lived in Maryville most of the time I was growing up. Then, I moved to Knoxville for college. I moved here a few years ago, after I graduated and got a job at the hospital in Maryville."

"Why not live in Maryville?" His questions are kind of rapid fire and I find myself offering up all the information, telling Gunnar anything he asks.

"My mother lives outside of town and I need to be close enough to check in on her."

"Is she sick?"

"No, a recluse."

Next.

Gunnar's eyes squint, but there's no judgment there, just curiosity. "Hmm. So, she never leaves her house?"

"Nope."

"Like, ever?"

"Never."

He nods and finishes the last bite of his blueberry donut. After he finishes chewing and takes a sip of his coffee, he continues. "So, what do you do at the farmer's market? Isn't that typically for farmers?"

I laugh, shaking my head at his assumption. "Farmers, gardeners, homemakers, artisans . . . if you have goods or services to offer, you can set up a booth."

"And what goods or services do you offer?" he asks with a quirk of an eyebrow.

"My mother's."

"The recluse?"

Biting back a smile, I nod. "Yeah, she makes beeswax candles and honey, and seasonal jellies and jams. Occasionally, she throws in some pickled vegetables. Basically, whatever is in season."

"I'm definitely going to have to check out this farmer's market," he says with all seriousness. "Sounds like it might be the most happening thing in Green Valley."

"No, that'd be the jam session on Friday nights."

Gunnar's deep, throaty laugh fills the diner and I'm entranced by him once again. "How did I know you were going to say something like that?" he finally asks, shaking his head.

"What about you?" I ask, wanting to turn the tables for a while and get the attention off me. But more than that, I want to know more about him. "Where are you from? What do you normally do for fun?"

It dawns on me, I already know what he does for fun and I don't like the answer, so I'm hoping he says something else I don't know. I'm enjoying this date too much to have it ruined by the reminder that Gunnar is a fighter.

"Well," he says, picking at a few crumbs on his napkin. "I'm from Dallas."

"Big city," I comment, trying to decide if that fits the picture of Gunnar I've been painting in my mind. There are a lot of things about him that seem very urban, like he's not from around here. He has a bigger-than-life air about him, so I guess it fits.

He smiles and nods. "I guess so."

"And for fun?" I prompt.

Gunnar shrugs, leaning back in his seat. "Concerts, hanging out with my friends. I just graduated from college back in the spring, so I haven't had a lot of free time yet."

"What kind of music do you like?" I ask, glancing at the lone jelly donut sitting on the table.

"A little bit of everything. As long as it has a good beat and good lyrics, I'm a fan."

I smile, because that's the same answer I would've given. "Me too."

Gunnar gives me that smile I claimed for my own again and it makes my insides melt a little.

"Wanna split this?" I ask, pointing a plastic knife at the donut. "You have to try the jelly-filled. They're the best."

I cut the donut down the middle and pick up half, handing it to Gunnar. When our fingers brush, along with the transfer of fluffy, flaky goodness is a zip of electricity. Kind of like during the winter, when it's cold and the air is dry and charged and you touch someone, shocking them. Except this didn't hurt, just caught me off guard, and from the look on Gunnar's face, he felt it too. The zing traveled through my fingers, up my arm, and all the way to the pit of my stomach, working itself into a ball of unfamiliar desire.

Gunnar immediately takes a large bite of the donut, distracting me with his fervor. I know the second the jelly hits his tongue because his eyes roll and he groans. "Oh, my God," he declares, looking down at the pastry like he's holding the holy grail. "I had no idea."

"I know, right?" I chime in, taking what feels like a decadent bite. I never eat more than one donut. Only one. And since I take it to-go, there's never a chance of having another. Except for today. I guess it's a day full of firsts. "You wanna know something else?" I ask, feeling brave and euphoric. Maybe it's the extra sugar rushing through my veins, or maybe it's the beefcake with the sea glass eyes sitting across from me, seductively licking jelly off his lip as he inhales the last bite of donut, but when he lifts his brows, encouraging me to continue, I blurt out, "I've never been on a date before."

Gunnar's hand pauses in midair and his eyes search mine. "Never?"

Shaking my head, I take another bite, filling my mouth so I won't have to talk. *Why did I say that?* I doubt it makes me more appealing or bodes well for my likeability. How can a twenty-five-year-old go her entire life without being on a date? The only logical answer is that she's not dating material, which would be true—but only because I've chosen not to be.

"Well, I've never had a jelly-filled donut," Gunnar says, like our two confessions are equal. "I've also never been to a farmer's market . . . or a jam session."

Smiling, I swallow the bite I've been working on and wrap my hands around my still-warm mug of coffee.

"Hey, Frankie," he says, drawing my attention back up to him. As he leans across the table, his hands coming dangerously close to mine, I hold my breath, waiting for whatever he's going to say. "Thanks for letting me take you on your first date."

The sincerity in his statement is so thick, I have to take a deep breath and let it wash over me. That warmth I felt thawing my insides earlier kicks up a notch.

Acceptance is a funny thing. Sometimes, I don't even think we realize how much we want it, or need it, until we get it.

Gunnar's acceptance of my truths I've entrusted to him mean more than I'll probably ever admit.

I want to tell him I'm glad he was my first . . . *date*, that is.

"What do you do after you eat a donut and get a coffee?" he asks and it takes me a second to realize what he means because I'm so caught up in him.

Clearing my throat, I try to sound unaffected as I answer, "I volunteer at a women's shelter in Maryville on Wednesdays and Fridays." Taking the last sip of my coffee, I glance up at the wall, noting that according to the clock hanging there it's now seven thirty. "Actually, I should probably be heading that way."

"Already?" he asks, shifting in his seat. "What time do you have to be there?"

"No specific time, really, but we're having a meeting today about some fundraising possibilities and it's kind of out of my wheelhouse, so I need to do a little research beforehand."

"I can help," he offers, catching me off guard.

I pause, waiting for him to say he's just kidding, but he doesn't, and instead, levels me with his serious gaze. "Really?"

"Yeah. I mean, I don't have a degree in marketing or anything, but I've been around my brothers long enough to pick up on a few things. We've done quite a bit of fundraising at the gym in Dallas. I'd love to try to help."

My shoulders sag in relief. I didn't realize how much this has been stressing me out until the thought of someone taking it off my plate makes me feel like I can breathe easier.

Give me patients with gaping wounds.

Give me people to help.

Give me chores to do.

But don't give me numbers and money.

I'm good with my own budget, but dealing with someone else's gives me hives.

"Helen, the coordinator at the shelter . . . well, she runs the place, but that's her title. She's everything... CEO, CFO, President, Vice-President, Treasurer . . . you name it, she's it—"

"What do you do?"

"I check people in, give them an initial exam, treat non-critical wounds . . ."

Gunnar listens thoughtfully, adding, "What you do best."

"Yes," I tell him, feeling that warmth spread through my chest. "I guess so."

"So, what does Helen need help with?"

I sigh, thinking back over our recent conversations. "The funding for the shelter has decreased over the past few years. It's privately funded and a few of the people who've always made large contributions have either fallen on hard times themselves or passed away. We need new donors, but more importantly, we need to recover the money missing from our budget for the year. If we don't, Helen will be forced to decrease the amount of people we can accept on a weekly basis. It's the only way to cut costs."

"So you need quick money . . ." he says, still thinking.

I didn't expect him to be so . . . I don't know—easy to talk to? I stare at him for a second, having a moment. How did I, Frankie Reeves, end up sitting across the table from this guy? And am I really going to let him help? When I met him in the ER a couple of weeks ago, I thought I'd never see him again.

He's different. Different from any other guy I've ever met, and different from who I thought he was. It's hard for me to rationalize the nice, normal, thoughtful guy sitting across from me with the violent, testosterone-driven fighter I'd built him up as in my mind.

He's not fitting into one compartment and that's hard for someone like me.

"Helen used to do benefit dinners and things like that, but those—"

"Are old news," he says, cutting me off. "People need something more exciting, more eye-catching."

Sighing, I lean my elbows on the table. "Basically," I tell him. "I've tried to think of something, but I don't have a lot of free time to sit around and brainstorm."

"Let me," he insists. "I'd love to help."

"But aren't you busy… training, or whatever?" I ask.

Gunnar shrugs. "Yeah, but I'm not doing it twenty-four hours a day, even though Cage would like me to." He smirks and I think back to meeting the two of them in the ER and how Cage worried over Gunnar with every stitch. He was worse than an old mother hen. It was kind of humorous seeing a big, burly guy like him pace the floor over his little brother, who isn't little, in any sense of the word.

"Okay, then," I agree. Digging into my bag, I find one of the business cards I keep on hand and pass it over to Gunnar. "This is Helen's information. I'll tell her today to expect a call from you."

CHAPTER 7

GUNNAR

"So, let me get this straight," Cage says, standing in the middle of the open kitchen as I fill two to-go cups with coffee. "You're going to the *farmer's market*?" He says it like I just told him I'm going to Timbuktu.

"Yes," I confirm, making sure the lids are on tight. The last thing I need is hot coffee spilling all over me before I can even get it to Frankie. I thought about stopping for more of those amazing jelly-filled donuts, but I decided it's better to leave those for Wednesday mornings.

Yes, I plan on meeting Frankie at Daisy's Nut House every Wednesday morning.

I've thought about driving to Maryville every other day and meeting her at the hospital for lunch or dinner . . . or maybe a midnight snack or whatever she'll give me, because I'm feeling a little deprived. How did I go my whole life without knowing her?

Now that our paths have crossed, I feel like I have a lot of time to make up for.

"Wait," Tempest says, jogging into the kitchen. "Did you say you're going to the farmer's market?"

Now, Cage is looking at her like she's crazy too.

59

"What the fuck is up with the farmer's market?" he asks. "Is it code for something?"

Tempest laughs, shaking her head and blowing him off. The way she looks at him—like he's the best thing since sliced bread, even when he's being a grumpy dick—is nauseating. "If you're really going, can I make you a list?"

"Sure," I tell her. If Cage thinks I'm doing something for Tempest, he'll stay off my case about being back anytime soon. When it comes to her, he'd rearrange the periodic table, if need be. "But I'm leaving in five."

She goes to one of the drawers and pulls out a pen and paper. "I'd go with you, but I have to be back at the bakery in just a few minutes. But if you could get me some of Ms. Reeves' honey, that'd be great."

"That's Frankie's mom," I tell her, wondering if Tempest knows anything about her.

"Really?" she asks, her head popping up. "I've never met her. Jenn usually picks up the things I need since I hardly ever get a chance to go."

"Apparently, she's never there either. Frankie picks up whatever she makes and brings it into town and sells it for her."

Tempest frowns, turning her attention back to her list. I could say more and I know she wouldn't judge Frankie or her mom about anything I tell her, but I decide not to. What is said between me and Frankie isn't anyone else's business, not even Tempest's. I already feel protective of her and even the simple conversation we've shared feels personal, because I don't think Frankie gives anyone much of herself. So, I plan on cherishing any little bit she's willing to give me.

"Well, tell Frankie to tell her mom I'd love more of the mint honey she made last year," Tempest adds. "I used it in some mint chocolate muffins and they were *to die for*."

"Mint honey?" Cage and I share a look, but it's not doubt. We know anything Tempest makes is to die for. Well, Cage knows more about her muffins than me . . . You know what? Never mind.

Thankfully, Tempest gives me her list and I shove it in my pocket, gathering the coffees and heading out the door. I really need a day out of the gym and away from the two of them. Have I mentioned I need my own place? Tempest mentioned the apartment she used to live in down the block is available. I have a little money in savings, and Cage is going to start paying me for teaching a few classes at night.

As soon as I have my first fight, I won't have to worry about it.

The few contracts Cage has received have me being paid, win or lose. That's the benefit of having my brother represent me, and of that brother being Cage Erickson. He knows it all and can do it all. There's also a lot of power packed in his name. Well, the Erickson name in general, but especially his.

Which is why I'm going to be able to pull off this last-minute benefit for the women's shelter where Frankie volunteers. After our date on Wednesday, I called Helen and she was on-board with my idea. When I hung up with her, I ran it by Cage, who got our brother Vali in on it, and in less than twenty-four hours, a Fight Night benefiting the Women's Shelter of Maryville was born.

Cage agreed it's going to be a great way to promote Viking MMA studio, effectively putting his name on the map locally. Vali thinks it'll also be great for me, since he and Cage are in charge of filling the ticket, they can make sure I'm fighting someone who'll give me a good fight but who I have a chance of beating. And it'll be the main event. Twenty-five percent of ticket sales will go to the shelter.

The venue we found in Maryville holds about twenty-five hundred people.

With the Erickson name attached, we should be able to pack it out.

At seventy-five dollars a ticket, which isn't bad for a benefit fight, we'll bring in around a hundred and eighty-five thousand dollars. It seems like a lot, but when you consider the costs of renting the venue, security, set-up, and tear-down, it's not. It won't leave much of a profit, but it will leave a good forty-five thousand dollars for the shelter—about ten thousand more than they need.

Helen was a little overwhelmed with the numbers, but quickly agreed to the plan. I told her the extra money could be put toward a special event or held over for operating expenses for next year.

Who knows? Maybe this will become a yearly event for Viking MMA and the shelter.

As I approach the community center, I quickly realize the farmer's market is more popular than I'd thought. Cars line the sides of the road leading up to the parking lot where the vendors are set up, and I have to squeeze between two minivans. One has a sticker in the back window that says, "Baby on Board." The other one has a sticker that says, "If this van's a rockin', don't come a knockin'."

Alrighty, then.

Still smiling, I cross the street with a coffee in each hand and Tempest's list in my back pocket.

It's a bright, sunny morning in Green Valley. The air is fresh. The sky is blue. And there's a pair of deep brown eyes checking me out as I walk up to a table filled with jars of honey and jams.

"Good morning," I say, squinting against the sun as I drink in the sight of Frankie.

She's got the cutest nose I've ever seen and it's kind of scrunched up as she cocks her head, hand going up to her brows. "What are you doing here?"

Looking behind me, I chuckle as I turn back around. "Well, according to the flyer at the Piggly Wiggly, this is the best place to find fresh produce, eggs, handmade soaps, and candles. And honey," I inform her, placing one of the coffees on the table in front of her.

"You brought me coffee?" she asks, her eyes flitting from me to the coffee and then back to me.

I smile, knowing I've earned myself a little bonus with the coffee. *Score one for Gunnar Elias Erickson. And the crowd goes wild.* Okay, that might be taking it a little too far. She accepted a cup of coffee from me, not a marriage proposal.

Whoa. Slow down there, buddy. We haven't even had a kiss yet.

What if she kisses like a fish?

No, not with those lips.

"Thanks," she finally says distracting me from my thoughts as she picks up the cup and takes a tentative sip. "I didn't have time to make any this morning. My shift went so late last night I thought I was going to have to call Gracie May to cover for me this morning."

My smile drops at the thought of showing up here to see her and her not being here. "Sorry you had to work so late, but I'm glad you're here to drink my coffee."

I made it just like she drank it on Wednesday at Daisy's—black.

"You made this?" Her brow raises in speculation as she takes another sip. "It's good."

I can't help the cocky smirk. It's not hard to make coffee, but I appreciate the compliment just the same. "Thanks." Turning to survey the rest of the vendors, I mutter under my breath, "I'd like to show you a few other things I'm good at."

"What?" Frankie asks.

"Nothing," I tell her, shaking my head. I take out the slip of paper Tempest gave me, needing to redirect my thoughts and this conversation so I can stick to my plan—keep Frankie engaged. I see her walls and I have a feeling they're not going to be easy to knock down. Even though I pack a punch, I know the hardest opponents take finesse. You can't go in guns blazing. You've gotta take it slow, look for an in . . . pace yourself. And sometimes, you have to woo your opponent.

Which is exactly what I plan to do to Frankie Reeves.

"I've been given a mission," I tell her, holding up the list. "Choosing to accept was a no-brainer because the reward is muffins. And I don't know if you've ever had something baked by the Duchess of Muffins, but they're—" I pause, kissing my fingers in a flashy gesture. "Delicioso."

That earns me a smile. "Oh, so now you're Italian? Or is it the muffins? Are those Italian?"

She's a smartass, and I love it.

"I'm Scandinavian," I boast, leaning forward so my hands are

63

resting on the table in front of her and my pecs flex. "Can't you tell? Blond hair, blue eyes . . . ruggedly handsome."

She laughs and it's the best sound I've ever heard in my entire life. "There's nothing *rugged* about you," she says, tilting her head up so our eyes meet. "You're kind of a pretty boy."

When her cheeks flush pink, I know she didn't mean to say that, but I love Frankie's unfiltered words. "Oh, really," I goad. "Tell me more about how pretty I am."

"I thought a big, tough guy like you would be offended at the term *pretty*."

"Pretty . . . handsome . . . it's basically the same thing," I say, smirking and leaning forward until our noses are mere inches apart. "Besides, a compliment is a compliment. So, whatever you want to call me, I'll take it."

"How about beefcake?" she drawls. Her words come out hesitantly, like she can't believe she's saying them, but there's no time to take them back. Now, it's my turn to laugh.

Throwing my head back, I let it roll through my belly and up my throat until I'm howling. "Beefcake?" I ask, still laughing. "Is that what you call me?" I've been called a lot of things in my life, but that's never been one of them. *Little Cage, Tiny Viking*—those were my nicknames in my formative years. Since then, I've graduated to *The Show*, a play off my name—*Gun*nar—and my muscles, as in gun show.

But never beefcake.

"Maybe I should tell Cage to put that on my next fight card? Gunnar *Beefcake* Erickson... it has a nice ring to it, huh?" Waggling my eyebrows, I earn another smile from Frankie and I decide I'm keeping every single one. I wish there was a way I could literally collect them and save them up for a rainy day.

She stiffens a little at the mention of fighting and I make a mental note to steer clear of that subject, leaving it for another day. "Care to point me in the direction of . . . Mr. Henson's blueberries?" I ask, glancing at the first order of business. "And make sure you put a jar of your mom's honey aside for me. Well, for

Tempest. She also wanted me to pass on that the mint honey she made last year was 'to die for'." I add in my own impersonation of Tempest Cassidy and thankfully Frankie relaxes, laughing at my antics.

"She just told me last week that she has herbs harvested and saved up for the winter. When it's cold and not much is growing, she loves to make her infused honeys and jams from the fruit and herbs she's frozen during the year."

The way she talks about her mother makes me wonder how close they are and if Frankie has any other family around. With her mom basically living in the woods and Frankie going once a week to check on her and take her groceries, who's there for Frankie when she needs someone?

Or does someone like Frankie never need anybody?

That thought doesn't settle well.

"Mr. Henson's booth is over there," Frankie says, pointing across the lot. "He should have a few boxes of blueberries left. I stopped by and bought some for my mother earlier and he had a lot."

When she looks back up at me, I see so much in those deep brown eyes—questions, indecision, curiosity, and yet she's so guarded. *What is your story, Frankie Reeves?*

"Do you want to go with?" I ask, pointing over my shoulder. "Maybe you could sweet talk Mr. Henson into giving me a deal on what he's got left?" I'm teasing about the deal. I'll pay whatever the man asks, but I'm not teasing about wanting her to come with me.

I want her, in every sense of the word.

"Uh," Frankie hesitates, glancing around. "I better stay here."

"Would someone seriously steal your honey?"

I almost say honey pot, but that makes me think of *her* honey pot and that's a downward spiral I can't afford at a family-friendly farmer's market.

She gives me a small, knowing smile. "No."

"Then you should come with me. It can be a second date," I say conspiratorially. "And I know you haven't been on one of those . . ."

She huffs out a laugh and rolls her eyes before groaning and reaching under the table. Placing an empty mason jar in front of me, she pulls a small sign out and sets it in front of the jar.

Honey $5

Jam $3

Candles $4

We operate on the honor system.

It's an old American tradition.

Don't screw it up.

"Nice," I tell her, nodding my approval.

"It's effective," she says with a shrug, walking around the table to stand beside me. Her scent is stronger today and not diluted with the sterility that usually lingers on her from the hospital. It's just pure, unadulterated *Frankie*—fresh, citrusy, and delicious.

As we begin to walk, she shoves her hands into the back pockets of her jeans, making me notice every part of her: ass, legs, the way she walks. There's an overwhelming urge inside me to wrap my arm around her shoulders and pull her to me. I need more. I want to know what she feels like and if it's as good as I've imagined. But I don't.

Slow and steady.

Pace yourself.

CHAPTER 8

FRANKIE

*O*n my drive into Maryville on Wednesday morning, I'm all smiles.

When I pulled up to Daisy's this morning for my Wednesday coffee and donut, lo and behold, who was waiting for me? Gunnar *Beefcake* Erickson. It wasn't a date, per se. We didn't plan it, but he was there and I was there . . . and we sat for over half an hour talking about mundane, random things. It was awesome.

He bought my coffee and donut again, sending a dozen with me to give to Helen and whoever else might want one at the shelter. It was a sweet gesture, and quite honestly, made me feel like a loser for never thinking of doing it myself.

Gunnar is definitely a charmer. But my inner skeptic wonders if it's a mask for something sinister. Or maybe that's the company I keep. There are several of the Iron Wraiths who seem nice, but deep down, they're just as horrid as the rest.

In my life experience, people always have their own agenda, and I wonder what Gunnar's is.

Does he truly want to get to know me?

Or am I a game? Someone who turned him down and he can't give up until he's conquered me?

Well, that kind of ruins my buzz.

As I drive a little more, thoughts of Gunnar revolve through my mind, just like they always do lately. And there is one thing I know about him: he's a man of his word. He said he wanted to take me on a date. He did. He told me he was going to come to the farmer's market. He did. He volunteered to help with the benefit at the shelter, and according to our conversation this morning, he is doing just that.

We never finished discussing the details, but he told me he spoke with Helen last week and everything is in motion, happening sooner than I ever would've been able to pull it off. Whatever they're planning is taking place in three weeks.

When I arrive at the shelter, I park my car in my usual spot and grab the box of donuts. Walking in, Helen is the first person I see.

"Good morning," she says, her smile is unusually broad. "Have a nice weekend?"

I frown at the small talk. Helen and I don't typically have a lot of small talk. We just get to work and get stuff done. Sure, we talk business when we need to, but neither of us require more than that.

"It was," I tell her. *The best weekend I've had in a long time*, I think, but don't say. That would lead to other details I don't feel like sharing, namely Gunnar.

"Your friend called me last week," she says, cracking the lid of the box and raising an eyebrow at the contents.

"From my *friend*," I say with a shrug, testing out her label for Gunnar.

Helen's brows go up in an unspoken question and I give her a roll of my eyes that says "don't ask."

"He's a nice man." Helen has never been one to reprimand me but she does let me know in her own way when she thinks I'm being too hard on someone or unreasonable. It's in her tone, and I'm hearing it loud and clear. As not to harp on the subject, she changes direction. "I think he's going to raise a lot of money for the shelter."

Setting the box of donuts down on the table, I fold my arms across my chest. "What exactly did he suggest?"

"Oh," she says, her eyes widening with something that resembles amusement with a hint of mischief. Helen might work in a church, but she's no saint. "He didn't tell you?"

I shake my head. "No, he didn't. All he said was the two of you spoke and came up with a plan. Then he changed the subject." Now that I think about it, he did get kind of tight-lipped when I asked, like he was avoiding telling me, but I wouldn't know why. If it's going to make money for the shelter, I'm all for it.

"A benefit fight," Helen says, laughing somewhat enthusiastically, like it's the best idea she's ever heard. "And the best part? He thinks we could raise over forty thousand dollars for the shelter. That's more than we need for the rest of the year. It'll give us the cushion we need for the holidays and then some."

Forty thousand dollars?

From one event?

"But a fight?" I ask, trying not to show my disgust—but I can't help it. "Is that even . . . *right?*"

"Why wouldn't it be?" Helen asks, her countenance shifting as she mirrors my stance—hip resting against the desk, arms crossed. "Do *you* know of anything we can do to raise that kind of money?"

"No," I answer honestly. It's the reason I jumped at the chance to have someone else work on it. "But a fight is so . . . *violent.* And we're a women's shelter who takes in battered women and children. That seems like a conflict of interest to me."

Helen rolls her eyes. "Oh, Frankie."

"Oh, Frankie, what?" I ask, following her as she walks off down the hall. "Tell me I'm wrong, Helen."

"You're wrong," she calls back over her shoulder. "It's a sport, Frankie. We're not throwing innocent women and children into a ring and letting someone beat up on them. They're all willing and able opponents. They train to compete. It's no different from a football player or a basketball player. If you know any other professional athletes, I guess we could call them and see if they can round up some of their friends and raise us forty thousand dollars."

She stops when she gets to the main room, sweeping a hand out over everyone eating breakfast at the tables. "Or I guess we can tell all of these people they'll have to find somewhere else to stay in a few months."

My eyes go immediately to Lisa and Allie. Lisa's face is no longer swollen and her cut is healing nicely. Allie looks happy as she and her mother share a peaceful meal. Everything about the two of them reminds me of me and my mother and my heart clenches.

"No," I whisper. "I don't want that."

Helen sighs, turning toward them. "It's not as bad as you think. You'll see."

We'll see.

I guess I can suck it up for one fight. I don't have to like it; I just have to tolerate it.

"I think he really likes you," Helen says, still facing all the mothers and children eating their warm breakfasts in a safe environment.

"Who?" I ask, playing dumb.

She laughs. "You're the smartest girl I know, Frankie Reeves, but that heart of yours has a lot of catching up to do."

CHAPTER 9

GUNNAR

"So, Vali will be here when?" I ask, grunting as I twist my body and throw my weight into a punch to the bag, and then repeat. Cage has amped up the training sessions since we put the benefit fight on the schedule. Even though it'll be for exhibition, he wants to make a good impression and earn some positive publicity.

From the other side of the bag, Cage replies, "Two weeks from Monday. Just in time to help us get the ring set up, since he's the best at it. I've found some guys to hire for the rest of the set-up. The venue provides concessions, so we won't have to worry about that. I'll be able to staff the doors from here. Everyone seems to be willing to volunteer their time. Cole is going to hook us up with some security. I think it's all coming together nicely."

"And on short fucking notice," I add, sweat dripping from my nose as I breathe through each punch, feeling the burn in my chest radiate through my muscles.

"For a good fucking cause," Cage shoots back.

Spinning, I switch to kicks and land a roundhouse that elicits an *oomph* from Cage as he holds the bag in place, ready for my next move. "It is." With my hands up near my face, I knee the bag and then switch feet to land a sidekick. "Thanks again for helping."

71

"The way I see it," Cage says, almost as out of breath as I am, "it's a win-win for everyone involved. You get a fight under your belt before we head to Nashville next month. Viking MMA gets some much-needed publicity. And the shelter gets the money it needs to operate."

"Frankie's pissed about the fight."

Cage holds the bag a little tighter, stopping me midair. "What do you mean she's pissed? I thought she wanted your help?"

"She hates violence," I tell him, repeating Frankie's words. "But I feel like it's more than that. I don't know. She's so guarded . . ." I think about asking him about the motorcycle guys that were bothering Frankie in the parking lot of the Piggly Wiggly a couple of weeks ago, but I don't. He hasn't lived here long himself, so I doubt he knows who they are. However, the questions have been burning in my mind ever since: Who are they? And what is someone like Frankie, who doesn't like violence, doing with them?

I've actually lost sleep over it lately, wanting to ask her about it but not wanting to scare her off.

"So how's that going to work?" Cage asks, drawing me out of my thoughts.

"What?" I ask, not following his question.

He cocks his head, leaning into the bag. "You and her. And don't tell me you don't like her because I won't buy it. You're head over heels for a girl who hates violence. Let that sink in there for a second, Gunnar *The Show* Erickson . . ."

I do let it sink it. I *have* let it sink in. Kind of. And I have no fucking clue how it's going to work, but I do know that I really like Frankie and I'm willing to find a way.

"What about the venue?" I ask, wanting to change the subject. "Are we confirmed?"

"Yeah," Cage says, stepping away from the bag and over into the middle of the mats. "They're knocking off about five grand, so we should come in under budget."

I nod, pacing as my heart rate continues to level out. "I threw together a press release and contacted local papers. Did you know Green Valley has a paper?"

Cage laughs. "Not surprising. This town thrives on gossip."

"I was also able to get in touch with a news station out of Knoxville that's going to add us to their 'Local Happenings' segment."

"Damn, maybe you did pay attention," Cage teases, ruffling my hair. I know they all thought I was the baby and not invested in the gym like the rest of them, but the truth is, I loved watching my brothers work together. And yeah, I paid attention, and maybe even learned a few things.

Side note: he's the only person on the face of the planet who could get by with ruffling my fucking hair. Well, him and my other brothers. No matter how big I get, even bigger than them, I'll always be the little brother and some things never change.

"Vali is going to die here," I say, using my teeth to rip off one glove and then the other, tossing them to the corner. Vince will be here later to spar, but I need a break. My hands are sweaty and if I don't hydrate I'll have muscle cramps later, and nobody has time for that. "There's not a Starbucks or Chipotle for miles."

Cage laughs, throwing a few kicks at the bag. "He's such a fucking wuss."

It's crazy; even retired, he could still kick my ass. There's so much power in every swift movement. His shoulder, which will never be truly healed, is the only reason he's not the reigning heavyweight champion in the UFC.

"Don't tell him that," I chuckle, thinking back to all the fights we used to get into when the five of us still lived at home. There was always a war going on between me and Ozzi. Viggo and Cage were always bossing everyone around, but where Viggo would leave me stranded at school to teach me a lesson, Cage would always come to my rescue. Vali a few years where we didn't see eye-to-eye on anything. Mom used to say it was because we were too close in age to get along, but one day, we'd all realize family is the only thing you're born into and will die with and eventually we'd have to suck it up and love each other.

We love each other.

All of us.

But it doesn't mean we always have to like each other.

Although, as we've gotten older, we've learned to put differences aside. Cage breaking away and doing his own thing kind of put a rift between him and Viggo and Vali for a while, but they're cool now. I mean, if they weren't, Vali wouldn't be dropping everything to come here and help with the benefit.

We need him though, and that's what family is for.

"How long is Vali staying?" I ask, squatting down and stretching my hamstrings.

Cage shrugs. "I don't know. He said it's good timing and that he was looking for an excuse to get away. Whatever that means."

"Who the fuck knows with him?" I ask, chuckling.

It'll be fun having another brother here to mess around with—I do know that.

I'm not sure this small town is big enough for three Ericksons.

CHAPTER 10

FRANKIE

*I*t's the sound that invades my dreams, turning them into nightmares. The same sound that chills my bones and rattles my nerves while simultaneously filling my chest with . . . what? Hope? Dread? A mixture of both?

The deep rumbling of the motors is only a couple of miles away but I know in my gut it's coming for me. Thankfully, I haven't driven out of Green Valley yet and can turn into a nearby parking lot and wait. Panic causes my heart rate to spike at the mere thought of inadvertently leading the Iron Wraiths to my mama's house, which is where I was headed before the sound of motorcycles invaded my peaceful drive.

That would be bad in so many ways. My mom would be furious if she knew I'd spoken to some of those bikers, but if she ever found out I've been helping them on occasion? Let's just say, my biker nightmares would pale in comparison to her reaction.

I put my car in park and wait. The radio is off, so the air conditioner is the only sound I hear outside of the thundering of my heart. Closing my eyes, I take in a deep breath and let it out slowly, willing my body to calm down. It works briefly, but as the roaring gets louder, signaling their proximity, my palms begin to sweat.

Sweaty palms have always been my tell, which made my clinicals in nursing school extra fun. The more experience I got, though, the more confident in my abilities I became, and my sweaty palm issue was almost completely eliminated.

Except for moments like this.

The bikes circle around my car while I stay seated, looking forward. It's not until there's a sudden tap on my window, scaring the shit out of me, that I realize someone has approached my car. I roll down my window and peer up at the man sneering down at me.

"Your services are needed at The Dragon. Right fucking now." The man practically growls at me. I recognize his face but I don't remember ever talking to him before.

"I can't. I'm late for an appointment." I guess there's not enough palm sweat in the world to keep my smart mouth closed.

"I don't give a shit about your plans. Follow us to the Dragon now, or I'll take you there myself."

When I don't answer right away, the burly man adds, "If you help us out in a timely manner, you just may see your daddy. Wouldn't you like that?"

This causes me to roll my eyes. "You guys have been saying that for years and I'm still no closer to knowing anything about my father. Why should I believe you now?"

"How do you know you haven't seen or met him yet? Maybe he's been at the compound all this time and you've just never noticed. That's not our problem."

I have wondered about that, actually. Although, I try not to look around too much when I'm at their place, I do occasionally glance at the faces near me just on the off-chance I see something familiar. A smile similar to mine, eyes the same color—anything that might clue me into whether or not one of those men was my father. And every time, I see nothing. Nothing happy, nothing caring or loving, nothing I want to be a part of and yet, I still can't seem to pass up the opportunity to try again.

Daddy issues much, Frankie?

"Fine. I'll help this time, but it has to be quick. And, if the wound is too deep or consists of something I can't treat on my own, you must take the person to the hospital, got it?"

"Yeah, yeah. Same deal as always. You follow me and the rest of the guys will be behind you, making sure you keep up. No funny business, got it?" His menacing eyes narrow, daring me to challenge him.

"Yeah, yeah. Same deal as always," I repeat, my tone taking on an air of boredom.

This time, I actually get a laugh out of him. "You sure would make a great Old Lady. You should reconsider our offer. It would be mutually beneficial, believe me."

I try to hide the shiver that ripples up my spine at his words but he knows my answer without me uttering a single word.

"Suit yourself," he says with a shrug before turning around and throwing a leg over his bike.

When he takes off, I fall in line behind him. The rest of the bikers do as he said they would and follow me as we make our way back out to the road.

Walking into the main building of the Wraith's compound does nothing to settle my nerves. If I'm being completely honest, it simply freaks me the fuck out. My mom is into Feng Shui and all that New Age stuff and even though I'm not, I can say without a doubt, this place reeks of bad juju.

Then why are you here, dumbass?

The compound is laid out like a very elaborate maze and, if I wasn't following someone, I'd for certain get lost almost immediately. Still, I take a few opportunities to look a little bit closer at the faces of those I pass just in case I see something interesting. Nothing stands out, as usual, and I swallow down the disappointment like I do every time I'm here.

I'm brought into a room with gray walls and only a mattress on the floor. On top of the mattress is a man who looks to be in his mid-to-late thirties. He's only wearing jeans, which helps me to identify his injury immediately. Bloody gauze covering parts of the right side of his chest and abdomen make me worry the wounds are too deep for me to stitch up. He may need surgery.

"When did this happen?" I pull gloves out of the medical kit I was handed when I arrived and quickly pull them on before lifting the dressing and assessing the injury.

"Last night," someone, I don't know who, answers.

"Why didn't you take him to the hospital then? You put his life at risk by letting him sit here all this time without proper medical attention."

"You wanna give us your phone number and home address so we can get you anytime we want?" A different man answers this time and I turn and glare at him. "I didn't think so."

I begin to inspect my patient, noting his wounds look more like lacerations than stabbings, so I rule out the need for a trip to the emergency room. "How did this happen?" I ask the man. Never in a million years would I have expected him to smile.

"Me and some of the boys were just playin' around. You know, wearin' blindfolds and runnin' around with knives. That kind of thing." The motherfucker has the nerve to shrug.

"Just an average night, huh?" This comes from the man who led me here and when he laughs, I fight the urge to vomit.

This is how they spend their time? Being reckless and violent and just plain stupid?

Forget scared or nervous, right now I'm pissed. "You all make me sick," I grit out.

"Hey, now," the man lying on the mattress says, lifting his head up to inspect me closely. "Why don't you just do what you were brought here for and shut the fuck up?"

I stand up and yank off my gloves. "Fuck you. I'm leaving. Have fun bleeding out," I tell my so-called patient before turning around and coming face to face with my captor—the man who summoned me.

"I guess finding your daddy ain't worth it." His voice is low and gravely and will most definitely star in my nightmares the next time I sleep.

"Worth what?"

"You've been coming here and helping out our guys for quite a while now and we've all been very impressed. You're earning our trust and that takes time, but once you have it, you'll be rewarded. So, you have to decide right now if finding your daddy means more to you than your pride. Cause if he does, then you need to get to work. If he doesn't, we're through here and you'll never get a fucking clue as to who he is or where you came from." He cocks his head, knowing he hit a nerve. That's all I want—answers to the missing puzzle pieces that make up my life. "You have about three seconds to make up your mind."

Why? Why do I need this so badly? Why do I even care who my father is? He, obviously, wants nothing to do with me and never has, so why am I putting myself through this just to be led on by these assholes? What if my father isn't even a part of the Iron Wraiths anymore? He could be long gone for all I know, and they could be using my weakness for their benefit.

I definitely wouldn't put it past them.

But I sigh in defeat, because regardless of what I do or don't learn about my father, my conscience won't allow me to leave the hurt man unattended to. So I swallow my fucking pride, put on another pair of gloves, and kneel back down. It's when I'm inspecting his wounds more closely that I notice a slew of silvery scars covering other parts of his chest.

Scars that look exactly like the ones on my body.

The scars I have absolutely no recollection of receiving.

Without thinking, I trace one with my fingertip and that's when I hear the screaming. Not from my patient, but from me. Not right now, but from when I was a little girl. Sitting back on my heels, I blink rapidly trying to clear it from my mind. The scream is so clear and audible, I look around the room to make certain there's not a child in here with us.

There's not.

Of course, there's not.

Trying to block out the sound—the only form of a memory I've

79

had at this point—I quickly patch the man up so I can get the hell out of here.

BC

It's not until Saturday at the farmer's market that I see Gunnar and when I do, I feel a sense of relief that should be surprising to me but isn't. I've been itching to call him or find him ever since I left the Dragon.

I've never really leaned on anyone before or had someone to vent to, but I wanted it after leaving the compound. And I wanted that someone to be Gunnar.

To be perfectly honest, I wanted even more than that. When I was finally calm enough to get into my bed and try to sleep, I imagined what it would feel like to be wrapped in his strong arms, with his mouth leaving sweet kisses on my head. I was so comforted by the images my mind conjured, I managed to fall asleep before my visions turned more X-rated.

I'm just full of surprises this week.

Still, I try to play it cool when he walks to my table. I cannot let him know I'm into him. Not yet, anyway. It's just too soon.

He greets me with a "Happy Saturday" and I try to bite back my smile because he already knows how charming he is. He doesn't need me to boost his ego.

"Hello. You already need more jam and candles?"

"No, I need more time with you and there are only three places I know you frequent besides the hospital on a regular basis, so here I am." He spreads his arms out wide and there's no denying the guy has an incredible wingspan. And muscles. Good Lord, he has muscles for days. They're lean, not too bulky, and look fantastic in his tight t-shirt.

"Wow, stalker much?"

Gunnar clutches his chest in mock horror. "You wound me, madam."

This gets a giggle from me and it feels good. Natural, almost. "Besides, you know a fourth place I frequent—the shelter."

"I know *of* the shelter, but I've never been there so it doesn't count," he clarifies.

"You should come with me one day." The words fall out of my mouth before I can stop them, but I realize I don't regret them. I want Gunnar to visit the shelter with me. I want him to see the side of me that helps others in a more relaxed environment than the hospital. I want him to see why the shelter is so important to me. There's also something else there, but I don't acknowledge it or the "why" behind my desire for him to know more about me. It's a foreign feeling and one I'm not ready to tackle today.

"Really? I can do that? I mean, you want me to go with you?" A flustered Gunnar is a cute Gunnar, and he's definitely flustered. My statement has surprised him more than it did me, and that's saying something.

"Yeah, I think it'd be great. You can see what the money you help raise will go toward."

"But, I'm a guy—a big guy. I don't want to scare anyone or make them feel uncomfortable."

Well, damn, I wasn't expecting that.

The fact he even considered the possibility his gender or size would undo the help Helen and I have given blows my mind . . . and maybe knocks a few of my walls down. There's definitely more to him than meets the eye.

"I love that you're concerned about that, but I really do think it'd be fine. I can run it by Helen first, if you'd like."

"I would like, and after, I'd like to take you out on another date *at night*. What do you say to that?"

"That sounds nice." A genuine but shy smile covers my face. I don't recognize myself at all in this moment. But something about opening up a little and taking a chance on this—on whatever this could be—feels good.

Just as I'm trying to put my finger on what's different about Gunnar Erickson and why I feel safe with him, he steps closer. The table displaying my mother's items for sale is still between us, but it might as well be made of water because it's not holding him back in any way. "You sure are amicable today. I kinda like it."

I don't respond. I can't. My mouth has lost the ability to form words and sounds while my eyes only seem to focus on his lips. He seems to be encouraged by my silence so I stay quiet, daring him to make a move.

So he does.

And so do I.

His lips are light as air at first, not teasing but gauging my reaction, and when a whimper escapes my mouth, he lets go of the restraint. Gunnar's mouth dominates mine and I follow his lead, gladly allowing his tongue access.

This man is absolutely delicious.

Too soon, he pulls away, forcing both of us to come back to reality. I can feel my face flaming with embarrassment because I've never let myself go like that, especially while out in public. And, although I can recognize what we just did was still fairly tame, it's still a big freaking deal to me and my small world.

Thankfully, no one around us seems to have noticed or care in any way about us kissing at the farmer's market. This being a small town with a big mouth, I'll still be shocked if this moment doesn't come back to bite me in the ass.

Gunnar clears his throat. "Um, that was . . . wow. Yeah." He shakes his head and I get the feeling he wants me to say something, but I can't. That kiss rendered me speechless. He's all on his own.

After a few moments, he finally collects his thoughts—that makes one of us—and says, "So, there doesn't seem to be as much product on your table as last week. Is, uh, everything okay with your mom?"

I'm grateful for the change in conversation and this bone he's throwing me for neutral conversation, but I wish he'd ask me anything but that.

It's true I don't have a lot to sell this week but the reason why has nothing to do with my mother and everything to do with my visit with the Iron Wraiths. After I left the compound, I was too emotionally drained to drive out to her house. Instead, I called her and lied, saying I had to be at work for an emergency. I, of course, have worked every day since then and haven't had time to go back.

But I'm not ready to share anything about that day with Gunnar. So I evade.

"Yeah, she's, uh . . . fine. Just a slow week. I'm sure she'll have more for me to sell next week."

He must sense the change in my demeanor, but in true Gunnar fashion, he's not deterred. Where most people would let it go and change the subject again, he persists.

"Frankie, you know you can tell me anything, ask for anything. Right? If you're ever *in trouble* or need help, I'm here for you—ready, willing, and able."

He's also entirely too perceptive. The way he says *in trouble* leads me to believe he's speaking about the Iron Wraiths without coming right out and asking about them, because he told me he wouldn't. So, he's keeping his word but still trying to get the information he wants.

If feels a bit manipulative and makes my defenses go up.

"Just because I let you kiss me doesn't mean you have the right to know everything about me. So, if that's what you're after, you might as well leave."

My words sound icy to my own ears, so I know they must sound that way to Gunnar.

I admit, it's kind of a shitty thing to say given the moment we just shared, but my stubbornness rears its ugly head and I clamp my lips closed, waiting for Gunnar's response.

Like hell will I be letting Gunnar get mixed up with the Wraiths. Not on my watch.

I'm the one who voluntarily goes into their compound, but I refuse to let anyone get involved with them on my behalf. Especially someone like Gunnar Erickson.

He and the Iron Wraiths just stink of violence, and although he looks menacing, I've come to know different. And there's only one of him and too many of them. If he got hurt because of me, I'd never be able to forgive myself.

The look on his face tells me everything I need to know. He pulls back as though I'd just slapped him and I instantly regret it. I should apologize and explain myself, but when I go to speak, Gunnar holds a hand up to stop me.

"No, that's fine," he says, his tone sounding just as hurt as his expression. Those sea glass eyes looking anywhere and everywhere, except at me. "I'll leave you alone, if that's what you want. Forget I said anything. I didn't mean to pry."

My fingers twitch to reach out.

My throat tightens with unspoken words to call him back.

But in the end, all I can do is stand there, watching as he walks away.

CHAPTER 11

GUNNAR

"To what do I owe this pleasure?" Cole Cassidy asks as I walk up the drive. When I mentioned to Tempest I wanted to talk to him about something, she was her usual self and didn't push for answers. She just told me he's off duty today and I'd be able to find him at home.

I smile and accept his hand for a shake. Cole is good people. I've known it since the first time I met him. I might be young, but I've always had a good bullshit meter and an ability to judge people. Not judge them for what they do or don't do, but gauge what type of person they are. My mom calls it a sixth sense.

Regardless of what it is, it's always served me well. Which is why I'm here.

"Hey man," I greet. "I just need some information, and you're the only person I know who might be able to give it to me."

Cole scrunches his face in confusion. "You've been in town what? A month? What kind of information could you possibly need? If you're here to complain about the speed limits or lack of stop lights, I'm afraid that's above my pay grade."

Laughing, I shake my head, wishing it was something as trivial as speed limits and stop signs. "I was actually wondering if you could tell me about a group of bikers I've seen around town."

There's no sense beating around the bush. After the way Frankie flipped the switch yesterday when I hinted around at her possibly being in trouble, it solidified my need to know more about the company she's been keeping. Even if she doesn't want mine.

"Bikers?" Cole asks, scratching his head. "We've got quite a few of them around here."

I can tell he's holding back on me and, quite frankly, it pisses me off a little. "You know who I'm talking about. Mean looking dudes, lots of leather, up to no good."

"The Iron Wraiths," Cole says, almost dejectedly.

"Iron Wraiths?" I heard him, but Iron Wraiths? *Really?* Is this like Green Valley's version of the Sons of Anarchy?

Cole glances behind him at the front door of his house and then back at me when he's confident no one is listening. "They're no good, man." His statement comes out hushed, like if he talks too loud one of them will materialize out of thin air.

Are they fucking Beetlejuice?

"I kinda figured that much," I mutter, running a hand through my hair.

"What do *you* know about them?" he asks, cocking his head.

I meet his eyes. "Not much more than what I told you already."

"Have you talked to them?"

Huffing, I start to get a little annoyed that he's jumping to conclusions about me and the *Iron Wraiths*. "No, I haven't talked to them, just seen them. And I think they know someone I . . ." *Like? Date? Want to date?* "Someone I know," I finish, not wanting to incriminate Frankie if these guys are as bad as I think they are.

"You don't want to have anything to do with them or anyone they're associated with," Cole advises, going full-deputy-mode on me. "Listen, I know you're new to Green Valley and it can be hard to find people to . . . hang out with, or whatever twenty-somethings do these days."

I want to laugh, because Cole isn't old, not by any means. Sure, he's older than me, but there's no way he's over thirty. I might've thought that was old a few years ago, but the older I get, the younger thirty sounds.

"If you want to find people to hang out with, try the jam sessions at the Community Center."

Laughing, I shake my head. "Are they as hopping as the farmer's markets on Saturdays?"

"You've been to the farmer's market?" he asks, disbelieving.

"Have you tried Mr. Henson's blueberries?"

To that, Cole quirks an eyebrow as if to say "touché." Switching back to the subject at hand, he says, "About those bikers—they're criminals, Gunnar. Not just your run-of-the-mill B&Es, but hard stuff. Drugs, grand theft auto . . . murder."

"Murder?" I ask, my mouth going dry as my stomach drops. *What the hell, Frankie?* Surely she knows what these fuckers are capable of, so why would she be hanging around them? It's on the tip of my tongue to ask Cole, but I can't. I won't out her like that. Besides, she basically told me to leave her alone—after the best first kiss of my *life*, mind you—and I'm still a little butt-hurt about it.

That kiss. Man, that kiss . . . it was everything and not enough all at the same time.

I've been dying to touch her. I didn't get much, but what she gave me was enough to make me an addict for life. And then she basically used it against me.

"Yeah," Cole continues, oblivious to my inner turmoil. "So, stay away from them. If you see them, go the other way."

Scoffing, I kick at the gravel beneath my feet.

"I'm not saying you can't take care of yourself," he adds, holding up his hands. He must take my reaction as one of offense, but it's nothing like that. I'm just so fucking confused as to why Frankie would willingly associate with these guys yet be so turned off by my fighting and be so guarded around me. It doesn't make any sense.

"I also know that Cage would kick your ass all the way back to Dallas if you get twisted up with these guys," Cole continues.

Now, that's the truth. Fighting for sport is one thing. Getting in a back alley brawl is another and it would earn me an economy class bus ticket back to Dallas. My father and all my brothers are sticklers about a fighter's code of conduct. The main one being no threat or use of violence.

Just because we can cause damage, doesn't mean we do.

Growing up, my father made it clear that our fists were only to be used in the ring. Or the cage.

That wasn't always the case in a house full of testosterone-filled Neanderthals, but we paid the price when we crossed the line. Usually, when we'd start fighting, my mother would stick us out on the front porch and lock the doors. Our entry back inside was a hug. It had to be longer than three seconds and we had to act like we meant it.

The one thing our father would allow was standing up for those who can't stand up for themselves.

Even though I haven't known Frankie Reeves for long, I know she's nothing like what Cole has described.

She's good, to her core.

She'd lose her own life before she'd take another.

Which can only mean they're either using her for their benefit or they have something she wants. Either option makes my blood boil.

BC

This morning, after an early training session followed by a long run with Cage, he tasked me with driving to Maryville to make deposits on the venue and rentals for the benefit fight.

I've done that, and now I'm driving around looking for a place to grab a late lunch.

Fine. I'm also stalling, because I want to drop by the hospital and see Frankie. I want to apologize for overstepping, even though that wasn't what I was trying to do. All I wanted was to let her know I'm here for her, when and if she needs me. She has an out, an ally, someone to lean on, even if she's not used to depending on other people—which I know she's not.

I want to be here for her.

While grabbing a sandwich at a small cafe, I remember the other part of our conversation from Saturday, when she told me she wanted to take me to the shelter. Since I have Helen's number in my phone and actually have a few things to talk to her about, I decide to call her up.

"Hello?"

"Helen," I reply. "It's Gunnar."

"Well, hello," she says, her older voice cheerful, but all business as usual. "How are you? Everything going okay with the benefit?"

"It's going great. I'm actually in Maryville today running some errands and thought about stopping by the shelter."

"That would be great." She says it so quickly, almost before I can get the statement out. It makes me think she means it and what Frankie said was true. "I'd love to show you around, give you an idea of where the money will go."

I'd like that too. Not that I don't already think it's a worthy cause, but when I meet with the television station and newspaper, it would be great to have first-hand information to give them.

Fifteen minutes later, I'm pulling up to an old church building. When I step out of the truck, I'm greeted by a woman carrying a clipboard. She has dark hair with streaks of grey in it and I'm immediately reminded of my mom. Unlike all of us boys—who took after our full-blooded Scandinavian father—our mother has darker hair and complexion. She always says she did all the work and our father got all the glory.

"You must be Gunnar," Helen says, approaching the truck with an outstretched hand.

I shake it and smile. "Yes, ma'am, I'm Gunnar Erickson. It's really nice to meet you."

"Likewise," she says, all business. "Let me show you around."

She walks me through the main rooms, showing me where the people who stay here eat and live. Some of the women are milling about, doing everyday tasks like laundry and taking care of children.

There are even more children in the yard out back.

Helen explains that some of the women have been placed with jobs and are gone during the day, so the shelter offers childcare to help get them back on their feet.

The building is old, but in good shape. It's easy to see it's well-cared for and I can only guess that is thanks to Helen, and people like Frankie who donate their time and services.

"This place is great," I tell her as we make our way back to the front of the church. "Seems like you're able to help a lot of people."

"We do what we can," she says with a sigh. "I've never had to turn anyone away, and it kills me to think we might have to start now."

My back stiffens with that. "You won't," I tell her, solemnly swearing it. Not on my watch. "You'll see. The benefit will go off without a hitch, and we'll raise enough money to keep this place functioning even better than it is today."

I was already on board before I came here, but now I'm one hundred percent committed.

"How did Frankie get involved with the shelter?" I ask, still craving any bit of information I can get about her. Since she's not very forthcoming, maybe Helen has a little insight for me.

Steel-grey eyes turn on me. Helen's no-nonsense expression hardens. "That's not my story to tell." Before I can process her statement or prod for more information, she follows it up with, "But Frankie has been around here for a long time."

. . . Frankie has been around here for a long time.

What does that mean?

Did she seek shelter here?

Is that where her hatred of violence stems from?

Was someone violent with her?

Do the Iron Wraiths have anything to do with that?

"Before you let your assumptions get the best of you," Helen says, stopping my overactive imagination in its tracks, "you should ask her."

Lifting my brows, I let out a humorless chuckle. "Well, that's a little easier said than done."

"She's a tough nut to crack, I'll give you that, but it's because she's had to be," Helen adds. "Give her a little time. Let her see she can trust you. If you say you're going to do something, do it. Actions will always speak louder than words, especially when it comes to Frankie."

Our eyes meet and I see nothing but sincerity there, and deeply rooted care. She's unknowingly answering my question from a week or so ago: *Who's there for Frankie when she needs someone?*

Helen.

Helen is there for Frankie.

After thanking her for her time and the tour, I promise to keep in touch over the next few weeks. She's going to collect some photos we can use in the media packets for our promotional push for the fight, and I told her I'd come by to get them next week.

I'd *thought* I liked Helen before I came here today, but now I know I do, especially seeing how much she cares about Frankie. With her words of encouragement ringing in my ears, I hop back in my truck.

There's one more stop I need to make before I head back to Green Valley.

CHAPTER 12

FRANKIE

There is no such thing as a typical day in the ER, but today has been oddly quiet.

On days like today, we try not to mention it, because as soon as we do all hell will break loose. Instead, we all walk around like we're busy, even when we're not. Everyone except for the Gossip Girls—Lana, Jodie, and Cynthia—who sit around in a huddle with lots of whispering and giggling. But that's nothing new. Even when we're in the trenches with blood up to our elbows, those three are still talking about who's banging who and who was caught with their pants down in the nurse's lounge.

When they say my name, I pretend I don't hear them, because I don't have time for that, even when I have nothing else to do.

"Frankie," a familiar voice says, getting my attention.

Turning, I see Gunnar standing by the door of the ER looking so damn good. But I can't enjoy it—him being here—because I still have a bad taste in my mouth from how we left things on Saturday. When I lashed out at him at the farmer's market to keep him from sticking his nose in my business, I didn't think it would end that way —with him walking away.

Honestly, I thought he'd rebound quickly and change the subject, like he always does. Gunnar is like rubber; everything bounces off him and he always seems to take things in stride. Everything except for my rebuff.

I didn't expect that.

But now he's here and I don't know why or what he wants or how I'm supposed to handle it, so I give him a tight smile. "Gunnar."

"Hi," he says, giving me a shy smile, which is very uncharacteristic of him. He's nervous. Maybe about being here? He's probably unsure of how I'll respond to him showing up at my work. My knee-jerk reaction is to brush him off; that's what I'd normally do. Not because I'm not happy to see him, but because I *am* happy to see him —so happy to see him—and that scares me.

But this show of vulnerability endears him to me even more. It softens my hard edges and chips away at the layer of protection I have around my heart.

"I was hoping I'd find you here . . ."

It's a question, which he's expecting me to answer, but I am suddenly very aware of the eyes on us. The Gossip Girls have abandoned their current topic. Marie and Dr. Cravat have stopped their quiet conversation. And they're all staring at us.

When I don't respond right away, Gunnar shifts on his feet, peeking around the door, and that's when he realizes we have an audience. And he smirks. To everyone else, he probably looks like the overly-confident person I first met, but that's not the whole story. Under the smirk and cockiness is a layer of insecurity, and that's what drives me forward.

Taking his hand, I guide him into an empty room. "I'm glad you stopped by," I announce, a little louder than necessary. "We need to check your . . . uh, stitches."

Thankfully, Gunnar doesn't hesitate and follows willingly.

"What are you doing here?" I ask quietly, eyeing the open doorway.

He smiles down at me, the first glimpse of the Gunnar I've come to know and . . . what? Like? The feelings swirling in my chest resemble a tornado; bits and pieces of my resolve are caught up with the emotions he makes me feel. It's strange and confusing, but nice. Better than nice. It's a bit euphoric—and that scares me.

I haven't stopped thinking about the kiss from Saturday. It has starred in every dream, awake or asleep. When I'm getting dressed and looking at myself in the mirror, my eyes focus in on my lips, trying to see the difference, because there must be one—some sort of sign that says, "Gunnar Erickson was here."

He staked his claim and will forever own the rights henceforth.

Kissing isn't something I've done much of, but that one was the best of my life. I felt it travel from my lips to my belly and then down to my toes. And I'd love nothing more than a repeat.

"I was hoping I could catch you on a break or something and buy you a cup of coffee." His voice a husky whisper. "I didn't bring any jelly-filled donuts, but I'm sure we could find something else *sweet* . . ."

The way he says "sweet" goes straight to my core and makes my toes curl in my shoes.

"But first—did you want to check my face?" His coy smile makes me bite my lip. Yeah, that was a really lame excuse. I know he had dissolvable stitches. I put them in. But he put me on the spot, and I worked with what I had.

Slowly, he sits on the edge of the bed and takes my hand to pull me closer.

Glancing over my shoulder, I feel my body heat up with that simple contact.

How is that possible?

I've never been one to be affected by a man. Sure, I've occasionally had needs and filled those needs, but I don't fall all over myself when a member of the opposite sex walks into a room. I can appreciate attractiveness in another person without wanting them for myself.

But not with Gunnar.

He's different.

Feeling hot and flustered and not myself, I quickly pull my hand back and smooth the front of my scrubs. "We should get that coffee,"

I tell him, fidgeting with the drawstring on my pants. "It's a slow day. And the coffee in the cafeteria is pretty good."

"Frankie."

"What?" I ask, looking back up and meeting his sea-glass eyes and wishing I hadn't, because now I want to drown in them.

He smiles again, reclaiming my hand. "I'm sorry for prying on Saturday—"

"No, don't be sorry." Shaking my head, I glance down at our joined hands and marvel at the way mine feels so safe and secure in his. How does a handhold feel so . . . intimate? "I shouldn't have been so . . ."

"Guarded?" Gunnar offers, squeezing my hand a little and drawing my attention back up to him. "It's okay. You can be guarded. That's your right. You can be whatever you want to be and I'm here for it. For you. That's the only thing I wanted to tell you. I'm here for you."

His words and tone are so genuine and sincere and it makes my chest crack, not in pain or sadness, but in relief and desire. He has no clue, but him giving me that out and the time to do things at my own pace makes me want to climb into his lap and lose myself in his warmth and protectiveness.

I don't even know where the thought comes from, but, yet again, all I can think about is how it would feel to have Gunnar's arms wrapped around me.

"Okay," I tell him, knowing he's expecting some sort of response. That's as good as I can do right now. Trusting people isn't my strong suit, but Gunnar is making it awfully easy. "How about that coffee?"

His eyes search my face and must find whatever they're looking for because a wide, soft smile forms and he brings both hands up to cup my face, reverently. For a second, I think he's going to kiss me again—*I hope he's going to kiss me again*—but instead, he presses his forehead to mine, and then his lips, before giving me what I really want.

Gunnar wraps his strong arms around my shoulders and embraces me.

It's different from any hug I've ever received before. It's different from the one I shared with Lisa, which was her taking what she needed and me giving in to it. It's different from the ones my mother gives me on occasion. She's my mother; it's almost a requirement. But this one . . . it's warm and strong and protective. I feel myself sinking into it.

Like the kiss, it's the best damn hug I've ever had—strong, reassuring, and warm. Just like Gunnar. His chest expands as he breathes deeply and it feels like he takes a part of me with him when he does. Closing my eyes, I imagine being encased in Gunnar and my insides melt.

"Let's go get that coffee," he says, standing but still holding me close. "Do you need to tell someone?"

Shaking my head, I clear the fog his presence brings and swallow. "Yeah. Meet me in the hall, okay?"

Nodding, he places another kiss on my forehead.

After waiting a few seconds for him to leave, I gather the covering off the bed while I try to do the same with myself. When I walk out, I briskly make my way to the bin where we put soiled bedding, which is basically any bedding touched by someone, and tell Marie, "I'm going for a coffee. I'll be back in fifteen."

"She's going to meet Beefcake," Marie mutters under her breath. I pretend I don't hear her and keep walking. She was the one who coined the term I've been using for Gunnar, but I don't like her using it. Now that I know Gunnar, I don't want her calling him that or thinking about him in that way. But again, I don't stop or say anything. I just keep walking, out the door and down the hall to where Gunnar is waiting for me.

His tall, *beefy* body is leaning against the wall, arms folded, putting his muscles on display. Even through his shirt and jeans, his physique is no mystery. Everything about him screams athlete. Since my talk with Helen last week, I've been trying to see Gunnar as just that—an athlete—and leave the fighting part out of it.

It's helped.

Getting to know the person behind the body helps too.

"Coffee is this way," I tell him as I approach, nodding down the opposite hallway. "It's not as good as Daisy's, but it gets the job done."

Gunnar pushes off the wall and falls in step beside me. "What time do you get off work?"

"Eight. I'm on the day shift right now, so I work eight to eight."

"Twelve-hour shift?" he asks, disbelievingly.

I nod, shoving my hands down into the pockets of my scrubs, needing to put them somewhere before I do something crazy like reach over and link my fingers through his. "Three twelve-hour shifts. And I get off at eight, as long as there's not an emergency or I don't have a patient I'm tending to. There's a bit of a grey area, but it all works out. And since I only work three days a week, I don't mind the long hours."

"But you don't just work three days a week," Gunnar comments. "You work three here and two at the shelter. Then you work the farmer's market on Saturdays and take care of your mom on Thursdays. When do you do something just for you?"

Giving a tight smile to a passing employee, a nurse from ICU, I scoot a little closer to Gunnar to allow her to pass and immediately regret that decision. The second our bodies brush, that electric current is back, making me feel things.

Desire.

Attraction.

"All of that *is* for me," I tell him as we approach the doors to the cafeteria. "Helping people makes me feel good. It's all I've ever wanted to do."

It also keeps my mind busy and leaves less time to overthink things and dwell on my past. I leave that part out, because even though I'm suddenly a wealth of information, I'm still not ready to completely expose myself.

Those flashes of memory that came surging back out of nowhere when I was with the Iron Wraiths last week haven't left. Sometimes,

I hear the screaming in my sleep and wake up in a sweat, but nothing else has come to me. No images to go with the screams. Only the screams.

And I know they're mine.

Well, mine, but from when I was younger. They're like glimpses into my childhood.

But why?

What would make me scream like that? And be so bad I'd block it all out?

That's the question I plan on asking my mother when I visit her this week. I need answers, and she owes them to me. I've been patient long enough.

Holding the door open for me, Gunnar looks down, meeting my eyes with his. "You're okay, right?" With the way he poses the question, I'm not sure if it's meant for me or him. Like maybe he allowed his inner thoughts to slip right out of those perfect lips. "Because if you need to tell me anything or . . ."

He hesitates and I know it's because of the way I shut him down at the farmer's market. He doesn't want to push and I'm thankful for that. There are unspoken words laced in his statement and it makes me wonder if he knows something.

What if he had his own run-in with the Iron Wraiths?

After they saw the two of us together, it's possible. I wouldn't put anything past them. Or above them, and definitely not under them. I realize now that by not telling him a little about them, I could very well be putting him in the danger I'm trying to protect him from.

Telling Gunnar about the Iron Wraiths will have to be another item on my list of things to do, right after I talk to my mother. If there's a way for me to put this all to bed before I tell Gunnar anything, that would be even better.

Besides, I don't want to talk about them right now.

They'd just ruin our third date.

"On Wednesday, after you volunteer at the shelter, I would really like to take you on that date we talked about. Maybe one that's not at seven in the morning or at a community farmer's market. And longer than fifteen minutes," Gunnar says, following me up to the counter. "Because Frankie, I'd really like to have some alone time." His words are close to my ear and pour over me like warm honey.

Yes, I think I'd like that.

Very much.

"Two coffees, please," I blurt out, needing a distraction.

Trisha, the cashier, gives me a shy smile, her gaze roaming over to Gunnar and getting stuck there. I don't blame her, but I don't like it.

Eyes over here, Trisha.

"You can put it on my account," I tell her, more to get her attention than anything. She already knows. I come down here every day I'm at work and order a coffee. But today, I have a side of beef and it's obviously so distracting that Trisha has forgotten her job. "No cream, no sugar."

That last line comes out a little more demanding, but it was either that or, "*roll your tongue back in and wipe the drool.*"

CHAPTER 13

FRANKIE

"*H*ave you seen Allie?" Lisa asks as she makes her way down the hall with a basket of laundry tucked under her arm. "She was supposed to be coloring at one of the tables in the dining room, but she's not there."

I recognize the panic on her face and immediately begin to explain, assuaging her obvious fear. "Oh, Helen found some sidewalk chalk and asked Amanda to take her and a few other kids out to the playground."

Lisa swallows and exhales, her shoulders relaxing a little. "Okay, yeah . . . that's okay."

"You okay?" I ask, taking a moment to evaluate, putting my nurse's hat on. Her color looks pretty good, but the dark circles under her eyes tell me she's not resting well. Maybe a talk with Helen or Pastor Davis would do her some good. The bruises have faded, and the cuts are healing. She'll probably have a scar or two, but nothing too noticeable.

Nothing like mine.

"Are you getting quality sleep? I could pick you up some melatonin, if you think that'd help."

I'm always a proponent of natural remedies when I know they'll work. My mother is a hippie, for lack of a better term—except for the hallucinogenic drugs, which I don't think she uses—and believes everything we need in life can and does come from the earth. I think it's another reason she's more at peace in the woods. According to her, she communes with the earth, and I tend to believe her. There have been days where I'd shown up to check on her and had found her in the greenhouse having full-blown conversations with a tomato plant.

I mean, who needs people when you have plants and trees and bushes that don't talk back?

"I'm sleeping okay," she says. "Well, better than I have in a long time."

But not great. I can see it on her face. The tired eyes and weary expression. She reminds me of my own mother; I've thought that since the first day I met her and Allie.

Part of me wonders if their presence isn't part of the reason tiny pieces of my memory have been creeping in. It's as if the combination of seeing them, the guy from the Dragon who had all the lacerations, and my own mental probing have all mixed together to dig up old bones.

And now that I'm getting a small taste, I wonder if I want them dug up at all.

Maybe they should stay buried.

But then I'd never know the truth, and something in me says I have to know.

My mother always says curiosity is my both gift and my downfall.

I think she's right. My need to know is what carried me through college and nursing school. And my desire to know more is what made me continue on to become a physician assistant.

That same desire is also what set my life on its current course, carrying me right into the lion's den . . . or rather, the Dragon Bar. And it's kept me going back, time and time again.

"Remember that Pastor Davis is available if you need someone to talk to. And Helen and I are always available, too."

She exhales loudly and turns her attention toward the playground.

"And you're safe," I remind her. "So is Allie." Sometimes women who come to stay here need to be reminded over and over this is a place of refuge and we take every precaution to keep them and their children out of harm's way. Some never truly feel safe and end up leaving, unable to stay in one place very long in fear of being caught up to.

Now that I'm older and have been around women like Lisa, I realize the reason my mother moved us from place to place when I was younger was because she was scared and never felt safe either.

"Thank you, Frankie," Lisa says, turning her attention back to me. "For everything. I mean it."

I smile. "You're welcome. And I mean it." Reaching out, I gently squeeze her arm, reinforcing my words—*you're safe, I'm here for you.*

Sounds kind of familiar.

Someone's been trying to convey the very same thing to me, but I've been too stubborn to accept it. Funny how life teaches us lessons in the most unexpected ways.

Lisa finally returns my smile and holds up her laundry basket. "I should go put this away while Allie is preoccupied."

"See you later," I tell her, walking into my office. I need to finish up some paperwork before I leave, and Gunnar is supposed to be back to pick me up in a couple of hours.

When I pulled into Daisy's this morning, he was there. But somehow, I wasn't surprised. It was like I knew he would be. Or maybe I'd hoped? Regardless, he was, and after a quick coffee and donut, he informed me he was driving me to Maryville.

He had some errands to run for the benefit and wanted us to be able to drive back to Green Valley together tonight, after our date.

A real date.

Sure, we've had a few, but this one is different. He's picking me up and we're going to a restaurant together—one I picked out. There are jitters in the pit of my stomach, partially because I realize there's no backing out. When Gunnar drove me to Maryville, he took out that option. He might've done it on purpose, but all the nerves in the world couldn't keep me away from this date. He's making me want things I've never wanted before, and as much as it scares me, it also piques that curiosity I was talking about.

What if?

What if I let myself feel all the things?

What if I let myself trust Gunnar?

What would happen if I let down my walls and allowed him in?

CHAPTER 14

GUNNAR

I'm being fucking ridiculous. It's just a date. I've been on tons of them and have never been this nervous before, so what the fuck?

I mean, yeah, this will be my first *real* date with Frankie—meaning I'm actually picking her up and taking her to a nice restaurant—but it's not like I don't know what I'm getting myself into. We've been seeing each other a lot recently and she seems to be warming up to me, which is great, of course. But there's still something holding her back. I'm trying not to push her; it's just hard to know where I stand.

Maybe that's why I'm so anxious. I feel like I'm being very open with my attraction to her and although I'm pretty sure she's into me, I'm afraid she might still walk away and never look back.

Me, on the other hand . . .

Regardless, I just want to spend time with her and show her a good time, whatever that means. No pressure, just fun. She says the time she spends helping others, whether on the job or off, is what she does for herself, but surely there has to be something she enjoys just for her. I'd love to see her throw some caution to the wind—grocery shop on a Friday and eat donuts on a Saturday. Shake things up a bit.

Do I think I'm the guy to show her how to do that? Hell yeah, I do.

When I pull up to the shelter, Frankie is already outside waiting for me. She seems even more nervous than I am and I hate seeing her like that.

"Hey." I greet her with a smile and a small bouquet of wild-flowers I picked up on my way here, hoping they ease some of her tension. "You look beautiful." She's always beautiful in a natural way—no fuss—but tonight I can tell she's made an effort to high-light some of her features, and she's absolutely breathtaking.

"You, too," is her reply and it's kind of awkward but only endears her to me more.

"I look beautiful?" I tease.

"Well, yeah. I mean, have you looked in the mirror lately? You know what your face looks like. Plus, you have your hair pulled back, putting it on display. It's not fair, if you ask me."

"What's not fair?" I try to keep the amused tone out of my voice but I can't help it.

"You and your face. It's not right to show off like that and make everyone feel inadequate."

Now, I can't tell if she's joking or not.

"Alright, enough of that." I grab her hand and pull it to my lips, waiting for her eyes to find mine. "This," pointing to my face, "is just a face. It's not perfect. I mean, there's a scar and everything." I give her a wink. "Yours, on the other hand, makes my heart skip a beat every time I see it. I don't give two shits about what anyone else thinks."

I place her palm against my chest, right where my heart is, and hold it there. I want her to feel the beats, the stutters, the pounding because she needs to know what she does to me. Her eyes grow wide and when she turns them back to me, I nod my head. "That's all you."

Frankie lets out a deep, shuddering breath and her body visibly relaxes. "I'm sorry I'm being so weird and anxious and insecure.

This is my first *really real* date and you show up with flowers, all sweet and gorgeous and—"

"Frankie." When she stops rambling and looks up at me, I continue. "Stop talking."

A look of surprise covers her face but my tactic works. I don't need her explanations, I just want her. Just to make sure, though, I lean down and gently place my lips against hers. She's so fucking soft and sweet and it takes all of my power not to deepen the kiss. When I pull back, she seems a little disappointed but calm, which is what I was going for.

"Come on, we have a reservation." I pull on her hand, leading her to my truck and helping her into the passenger seat.

It's not until I've pulled onto the highway that she speaks again. "Thank you for the flowers. They're beautiful."

"You're welcome."

"What made you choose wildflowers?"

"Well, I wasn't sure what your favorite flower is and I didn't want to get you something typical or cliché. These, though . . . I don't know, they reminded me of you. Beautiful, colorful, and full of life."

"That doesn't sound like me."

I give her as stern a look as I can while driving. "You are all those things. You're a wild child, Frankie Reeves. You just need to be set free."

"I suppose you think you're the one to help me with that?"

"Damn straight."

BC

"I've lived around here my entire life, but I've never eaten at The Front Porch," Frankie says as we both look over our menus.

"Really? From what I hear, this is the nicest restaurant in town. I know you didn't date, but what about with friends for prom or home-coming or whatever?"

She shakes her head, not looking at me. "No, I never went to any of those either."

"Why not?" It's hard for me to imagine Frankie being a typical teenager but surely, she must have had some kind of social life. "What did you do for fun?"

"Same as now, I guess." Frankie shrugs but I can tell her eyes aren't focused on anything. She looks as though she's lost in a memory so I give her time to continue her answer. "My mom didn't want me hanging out with local kids, and besides that, we moved around so much, I didn't really have any friends to hang out with. It was somewhat better when I was at college."

"Only somewhat?" I'm trying to keep my reactions neutral but it's a struggle. All I know is I want her to keep talking.

"It was quite the adjustment going from a sheltered kid to an adult with freedom. Plus, my social skills were lacking, to say the least. I'm a quick learner, though, and I did the best I could. Now, here we are."

Her cheeks are flaming red and she still won't look me in the eye, so I reach out and grab her hand. I watch as her eyes close, realizing how truly difficult this must be for her, and my heart aches. I give her hand a squeeze and whisper, "For what it's worth, I think you're amazing." Her eyes close tighter and her chin wobbles, so I try another tactic because the last thing I want is for her to cry.

"When I was a freshman in high school, we had to wrestle in PE class. One day, I had to wrestle a girl, which was fine by me, until she accidentally slipped her hand up my shorts and grabbed my balls. I guess you could call it my first hand job, only it wasn't as enjoyable as I would've hoped."

Frankie lets out a loud snort before covering her mouth. "That really happened?"

Placing my hand over my heart, I answer. "I swear it did. A couple of years later, I took that same girl to the Homecoming dance. I was very pleased to learn her technique had improved immensely."

"Oh, my gosh. You're terrible, you know that?" Frankie wipes at her eyes, but I'm relieved the tears are from laughing and not crying.

After a fantastic meal and even better company, I reluctantly drive Frankie to her house and turn the truck off. I don't expect her to invite me inside her place. We're still moving slow, and that's okay.

"You really didn't have to drive me home," she says quietly before turning her gaze to me.

She's right, I didn't, but I wanted to make sure she made it home safely. And more than that, I wanted more time with her. "I wanted to," I tell her. A bonus to driving Frankie home tonight is getting the privilege of taking her back in the morning.

"Thank you for tonight, Gunnar. I really had a great time." She unbuckles her seatbelt and turns her body sideways to face me. "It was the best first real date I've ever had." Her smile is blinding and I return it with my own. A few weeks ago, I would've never thought she'd give me a smile like that, but now that she has, I want more. More smiles, more expressions. I want to know her moods and what she's thinking simply by the look she gives me.

"The date isn't technically over, you know. I believe there's a kiss that needs to happen."

"Oh, so I'm obligated to kiss you just because you bought me dinner?"

"Certainly not," I answer. "But I am hoping you'll allow me to show you how much I enjoyed our date by letting me kiss you."

She bites down on her lip to keep from smiling as she pretends to think about my offer. Finally, she gives me a sly grin and says, "I guess that'd be alright."

I don't give her a chance to change her mind—not that I think she would. I reach for her, one arm sliding around her waist while the other hand cups her jaw and pulls her mouth to mine. There's no testing boundaries like at the farmer's market; there's only intense, passionate kissing and I can't get enough.

It's as if a switch has been flipped within Frankie.

If she's this wild while making out in a truck, I can't wait to find out how she is in bed.

She pushes my shoulders back and moves to straddle my lap. I grab for the lever at the side of my seat, pulling it to move the seat as far back as it can go to give us more room. Once that's done, Frankie settles on top of me and holy fuck . . . I can feel the warmth between her legs wrap around my throbbing cock and we still have our freaking clothes on. By the way her eyes are glazing over, it's obvious she feels it too. When my dick involuntarily twitches, she gasps.

This feels like the night I lost my virginity—all the newness and excitement, the fear of blowing a load in my jeans before anything important happens. But it also feels like so much more than that. I'm as turned on as I've ever been in my life but all I care about is how Frankie feels, what she's thinking.

"Can I take your hair down?" she asks, catching me off guard.

I huff out a laugh. "Honey, you can do anything you want to me."

She carefully pulls the rubber band out of my hair before slipping her fingers through the strands. "I've been wanting to do this all night," she admits.

The initial urgency of our make-out session has faded, leaving behind a charged energy that's more controlled but every bit as intense as before. I have to kiss her. So, I do.

Frankie immediately accepts my tongue in her mouth and groans her pleasure when our tongues touch. Eventually, my need to taste her skin overtakes me and I take my time nipping, licking, and sucking my way across her jaw and down the column of her throat. When I reach her collar bone, my hands tighten around her ass and rock her against my length.

"God, Frankie, I want you so bad," I murmur against her earlobe, just before I suck it into my mouth. She sighs contentedly so I continue sucking on her lobe as my hand travels to where her shirt is raised just a bit. It's just enough to entice me with her soft, pale skin.

Remember that switch I mentioned earlier? Well, it just flipped again—but this time, in the opposite direction. Frankie's body freezes and she's no longer soft and pliable in my arms. She's rigid and tense and I fear I've done something really wrong. I just don't know what.

"I have to go," she spits out.

"O—okay," I stammer, trying to keep up with her shift in moods. "Are you okay? Did I do something wrong?"

I watch, helpless and confused, as she climbs back to her seat, straightening her clothes and taming her hair.

My mind is racing with explanations, but I can't wrap my brain around any of them. Did I cross a line? Do something she's not comfortable with?

When she wipes her mouth, I feel my stomach drop. It's bad enough she won't talk or even look at me, but to see her wipe away all evidence of us—*me*—it feels like I've been kicked in the gut.

No, worse. It feels like I've been kicked in the heart.

"Frankie?" I ask tentatively. "What's wrong?"

She shakes her head as she opens the car door. "I'm sorry," she says quietly. "I have to go."

CHAPTER 15

GUNNAR

*P*unching the bag, I let the sweat drip down my face and relish in the burn of my muscles. I need this. I need an outlet for the frustration that's been building, especially after last night.

Frankie and I had the best date ever. Dinner was awesome. We talked. She started to open up. That amazing chemistry between us was at an all-time high, and when I finally felt like we were finally on the same page . . . *wham*. Door shut. Walls up.

She just shut me out.

"Whoa," Cage says, walking down the stairs into the studio. "Save that kind of energy for the ring, little bro."

Pausing my assault on the bag, the same one that brought Frankie into my life, I wipe my forehead with the back of my arm and take some deep, cleansing breaths.

"What's up?" he asks, his brows furrowing as he takes me in.

Shaking my head, I catch my breath and let the sweat continue to drip.

"Something is," he continues. "Spill it."

Sometimes, I hate how well he knows me. It doesn't leave much room for privacy. Having four brothers of varying ages and me being the baby has meant I've lived my life in the open, never getting to keep much of my thoughts to myself. I've been pretty tight-lipped about Frankie, not giving away much information except for what little everyone else in town seems to know about her. The rest of it has felt private, like something she's entrusted me with. I refuse to betray what little trust she's given me.

"It's about the girl, huh?" Cage presses. "Frankie?"

Fuck.

I hate it, and yet, somehow, I love it too. Because I'm out of my league here and I need some advice. Cage has always been my sounding board, the person I can go to, regardless of the situation. Except for relationships; I've never needed him in this arena. For one, Cage was never the relationship type until Tempest. And I've never been much of one myself, until Frankie.

Two peas in a fucking pod.

"She just keeps shutting me out," I finally breathe out, hands on my knees. "Every time I think we're making progress, she brings these fucking walls up that are so thick, I can't see through them or over them . . . nothing. And last night, things were, well—"

"Heating up," he supplies, quirking an eyebrow, insinuating far more than what actually happened.

"Yeah," I say, shaking my head, because I have no desire to tell him details about that. I definitely don't need advice in that area. Not to be cocky or anything, but I know exactly what to do with my dick when given the chance. It's the rest of it that has my mind muddled. "But she threw the fucking brakes on so fast I got whiplash. One minute, everything is fine. The next, she's walking away and I'm left scratching my head, wondering what the hell happened."

"With blue balls to boot."

Rolling my eyes, I huff. "Yeah, okay, fine, the bluest of blue balls, but that's not my biggest concern."

That title goes to Frankie Reeves.

What the fuck is going on with her, or happened to her, that she's so unwilling to let me in?

"You should just cut your losses, man. Walk away."

This makes me jerk around and look at him like he's lost his damn mind, but that doesn't stop Cage. He keeps rattling off bullshit.

"I've known girls like Frankie Reeves and they're more trouble than they're worth. If she was into you, you'd know by now. Maybe she's stringing you along for the fun of it. You know, there are chicks out there who get a kick out of shit like that. Like this one girl I hooked up with for a while back home—one day, she'd act like I was her favorite person. The next day, she would pretend like she wasn't interested. Come to find out, she was playing fucking games. She'd been burned so much, leading men on was her way to *get revenge*."

He says that last part with air quotes and I feel a fire ignite in my stomach. Frankie is nothing like that. I know people. I read people. And no matter how she acted last night—or any time before that— one thing I know for sure is Frankie isn't out to hurt me. If anything, she's trying to keep herself from being hurt . . . and maybe me too.

"Cut your losses," he reiterates. "You don't need that kind of distraction in your life right now."

The fury must be written all over my face as we lock eyes. Cage lets his words simmer and I try not to lose my shit. The protector in me wants to pound his face in for even speaking about Frankie like that. I want to rage. *He doesn't know her.* He doesn't know what he's talking about. But then I see the shift in his demeanor, the slight change of features—going from stern to understanding.

He recognizes something in me, like a reflection in a mirror.

"Unless . . ." he starts, pausing. "Unless there's something more there. Then I'd say fight for what you want. But don't let her come between you and the progress we're making here. If this is still what you want . . ."

If this is still what I want.

It is, right?

I want this.

It's all I've ever wanted, what brought me to Green Valley.

But now, I want something else too—Frankie Reeves. She's worked her way under my skin and into every fiber of my being.

"A piece of advice," Cage says, letting me think and not asking me for anything. That's my big brother. "She might need you to put it all out on the line for her. Some people need that. They need to know if they fall, someone will be there to catch them."

I can't let things end like this, not without putting it all out on the table first.

Thankfully, since I drove Frankie home last night and then picked her up this morning to take her back to Maryville, I now know where she lives. So, after my training session is over, I run upstairs and shower and throw on an old pair of jeans and an Erickson MMA t-shirt. It's old, and a little small, but since it's been washed a million times and stuck with me through high school and college, it's my favorite. I always find myself wearing it when I need a little comfort.

Yes, even big, tough MMA fighters need comfort from time to time.

This is one of those times.

Shoving my wallet in my back pocket, I grab my phone and head down the stairs. It's not until I'm in the truck that I realize it's still relatively early and I have no clue how long Frankie stays with her mom on Thursdays.

To buy myself a little more time and keep my mind from going off-course, I stop by Daisy's Nut House for some donuts. It never hurts to come bearing gifts; anything to help break the ice around Frankie's heart.

When I pull up in the parking lot, I see a few bikes parked side by side and I immediately get a rush of adrenaline and my head feels a little lighter, like it does before a fight. Brushing my hair back, I grab a rubber band from my pocket and tie it back. It's a nervous habit and probably why I don't cut too much off.

These could be any bikes . . . any bikers. But thanks to my conversation with Cole and what little I now know about the Iron Wraiths, I'm on edge.

Walking into the diner, I let my eyes roam until they land on a table full of guys in leather. I don't recognize any of them from the night they had Frankie cornered in the Piggly Wiggly parking lot, but that doesn't mean anything. It was dark and I was more focused on her than them.

An unfamiliar face is at the counter when I place my order, but that's probably because I've never been in here at this time of day. "Four jelly-filled donuts, if you've still got some."

"You're in luck," the girl says. "We normally don't, but it was an unusually slow morning."

She grins at me as she goes to grab my donuts and I offer a polite smile in return, but then quickly focus my attention back to the table of bikers. When one turns in my direction, I don't avert my gaze. If he recognizes me, I want him to know I'm not scared of him.

He squints and I can't tell if he has trouble seeing or if it's supposed to warn me off. Whatever is the case, I still don't look away.

A few seconds later, he turns back to the other two sitting at the table with him and they begin to discuss something quietly, but never look back at me.

"Four jelly-filled donuts," the chipper girl says, handing me a bag.

"Thanks," I say, pulling out cash to pay.

She catches my line of sight and looks over her shoulder. "Don't worry about those guys. They're pretty harmless."

"You know them?"

Shrugging, she says, "Everyone does, but I don't let them get to me."

"Iron Wraiths?" I ask. Her eyebrows shoot up.

"Yeah, but I like to pretend they're just regular ol' nobodies."

Smirking, I nod. "Good thinking."

Regular ol' nobodies who have something to do with my girl. Yeah, my girl. Frankie is mine until she point-blank tells me to go jump off a cliff. I know there is something between us. I can feel it. I can read between her lines. I'm starting to learn her nuances and I want to know more. I want to know everything, including what those fuckers have to do with her, what they want with her.

Giving them one last scathing look, I turn back to the girl.

"Thanks," I say, holding up the bag and not missing the way she looks at me and then back to the table of bikers. There's a warning in her glance that says, "Don't poke those bears."

I'm not planning on it, but I also want them to know there's someone new in Frankie's life and he's not going anywhere. Not yet, anyway.

When I pull into Frankie's drive, her car isn't there. Taking out one of the jelly-filled donuts, I eat my feelings while I wait.

It's over an hour before I see her Mustang turn at the corner and then move slowly up to her drive. If her approach is any indication, she's not happy to see me here.

Reluctant, at best.

Stepping out of the truck, I shut the door behind me and wait for her to get out of her car. She takes her time and that's fine. I'm willing to take this as slow as she wants, as long as she allows me to stay.

When she finally gets out of her car, she walks around the front and mimics my stance, similar to that night in the Piggly Wiggly parking lot: arms crossed, back against her car. We both sigh, but neither speak for a few moments. It's not awkward, and for that I'm thankful. It's just quiet, thoughtful.

"I brought you these," I tell her, reaching through the open window of the truck and retrieving the donuts. "There were four, but I ate two while I was waiting."

This earns me a smile. It's small but it's there.

"I also wanted to apologize for—"

"Don't," she says, cutting me off and turning her gaze toward the road. "Don't apologize. It's not—"

"Please." I'm the one who cuts her off this time, my heart plummeting to my stomach as I hear the words before she ever gets a chance to say them. "Please don't say, 'It's not me, it's you,' because that sounds a lot like goodbye and I don't think you really mean it."

Her eyes go wide, and they stick to mine like glue as she hangs on every word I say.

"I came here today to tell you I'm sorry if things escalated too quickly last night, but I need you to know as much as I want you . . ." I pause, wanting to reach for her but deciding a little distance is good. There are things I need to get off my chest and when I'm touching Frankie all coherent thoughts seem to take a back seat. "I do want you, so much, but I'm willing to take this slow. As slowly as you need. It's not just a physical connection I feel or want with you," I admit, reaching up to smooth errant hairs out of my face. "It's everything, Frankie. The good, the bad, and everything in between."

She blinks—once, twice, three times—and then swallows.

When she doesn't respond after a few moments, I ask her something that's been bothering me since last night. It's a conversation I haven't had with a woman in a long time, but I feel like I need to have it with her to clear the air, so to speak. After lying in bed for hours last night, it's the one thing that kept popping into my mind. It could be where her hesitation comes from, and I need to know. "Are you a virgin?"

This pulls her out of the fog that seemed to settle over her and she lets out a rough laugh, shaking her head and putting me at ease a little. Not that I wouldn't want to be her first, because that would be a lie. When I say I want everything with Frankie, I mean everything —her firsts, her lasts, whatever she'll give me.

"No," she says, her voice sounding a little raspy, weak. It's then I realize she's wearing scrubs and looks tired. She doesn't look like someone who had the day off visiting with her mother. "I'm not a virgin. I haven't been for a long time. Since I was seventeen, actually. I wanted to know what all the hype was about, and basically coerced a guy in my study group to have sex with me."

Now, that's funny and I laugh. "There's no way in hell any guy would have to be *coerced* to have sex with you."

She lifts an eyebrow. "Well, I've never been good at relationships."

"Have you ever…" What? What am I trying to say? Has she had a boyfriend? Of course, she has. I know she's never been on a date, but no twenty-five-year-old who looks like Frankie Reeves has made it through life without a boyfriend. Surely there's at least been that, right?

"I've never been in a relationship," she admits, and I practically swallow my tongue.

Shifting on my feet, I place my hands on my hips. "Never?"

Shaking her head, she tightens her arms around her stomach and I hate it. It's like she's trying to hold herself together, but I don't want her to feel like that around me. If she needs someone to hold her together, I'll do it. I'll be here for her, no judgment, regardless of her past or present. I don't care if she's never had a boyfriend or if she's had a million. All I care about is that right now, she's with me.

"I've had one-night stands with no strings attached. That's it. Which is why this," she pauses, motioning between us. "This connection I feel with you . . . it scares me. I don't know what to do with it. Everything in my life fits in a compartment in my brain, but you . . ." She huffs, hanging her head and taking those gorgeous brown eyes from me.

Needing to see her, to know exactly what she's feeling, I bend down, searching for her. "What about me, Frankie?" I ask. She looks at me with so much emotion. Hurt, longing, needing, hopefulness, hopelessness—everything is swirling in her eyes like a violent storm.

"You take up all the space," she admits. "You don't fit in a compartment."

Without another word, I stand and wrap my arms around her shoulders, pulling her into my chest. It's my new favorite thing—having Frankie close. She fits so perfectly with my chin coming to rest comfortably on the top of her head. It's like she was made for this; made for me.

I'm not sure how this happened. Frankie came into my life so unexpectedly, but now that she's here, I know there's no walking away. I also know it's not going to be easy, but I'm willing to stick around and wait for every last piece of her walls to crumble.

CHAPTER 16

FRANKIE

These past couple of days have been, well, weird.

My date with Gunnar on Wednesday was everything I hoped it would be and more.

Then everything went to shit. When he drove me home and we started making out in my driveway, I wanted it. I wanted him. But my stupid brain started filling up with all the self-doubts and insecurities—the scars, my inability to have a relationship, the past I'm struggling to remember.

How could I tell him that stuff in the heat of the moment? But then again, how could I not?

Just as Gunnar's hand slipped under my shirt, skimming softly along my abdomen, I froze.

If his hand had traveled to my back, he'd have been able to feel the scars that lined the skin. They're not as prevalent as they once were—over time they've stretched and faded—but they're still there. Faint, but noticeable. And then there are the ones on my legs, which I never allow to show.

It was too much.

I couldn't compartmentalize any longer, so I bailed. I reached for the handle and stumbled out, leaving Gunnar a confused mess in the front seat. I told him to go.

So he did.

Just like I knew he would.

Because first and foremost, Gunnar is a gentleman.

Then, on Thursday morning, as I was getting ready to go visit my mother, I got a call from the hospital telling me they were short-staffed and needed me. Unlike my previous shift, everything was complete chaos. It started with a ten-car pile-up that filled our entire ER with patients and ended with three men who'd been in a knife fight.

For a second, when the call had first come in, fear had rushed through me, wondering if somehow the patients coming in were part of the Iron Wraiths. Thankfully, they were a few teenagers who were probably in some sort of gang. That's not my job to determine. I just patched them up and let the cops do the rest.

When I got home, Gunnar was waiting for me in my driveway and his vulnerability once again made my walls come crashing down. I still don't know what I'm doing when it comes to him. This is all such uncharted territory, but his patience and care are every-thing I never knew I wanted.

On top of all that, I slept like crap. These pieces of my past—of my childhood, the things I've tried so hard to remember all these years—are creeping in like ghosts in the night, invading my dreams. This morning, I woke up in another heap of sweat and twisted sheets, and not for any good reasons . . . like me and Gunnar having sex.

Although, I've thought about that possibility a lot since the driveway incident.

I'm a mess.

To make matters worse, I was running late and didn't have a chance to make coffee or stop at Daisy's for a cup. So, I'm sleep-deprived, frazzled, and under-caffeinated.

As I drive into Maryville, I think about stopping at one of the coffee shops in town, but decide Folgers will have to be good enough this morning. Helen always has a pot made.

Turning off the main road onto the side road that leads to the shelter, I pause when I see a woman and child walking down the street ahead of me. Even from this distance, I can make out familiar blonde hair and the girl is wearing a pink shirt I recognize.

Then, I realize they're walking fast and Lisa turns to look at the truck pulling up behind them. I'm almost two blocks away when the truck stops and a man gets out, forcing them into the cab.

My heart jumps as my foot presses on the pedal.

NO.

He can't do that.

He can't just take them and drive off.

When they turn down another side street, I speed up to follow them. The truck drives erratically until he veers off onto the shoulder, and I'm afraid he's going to overcorrect and flip. The thought makes me panic and I reach for my phone that's in the passenger seat.

Frantic, I try to keep one eye on the road as I dial 9-1-1.

"9-1-1, what is your emergency?" a lady from the other end of the line asks.

I'm quickly losing the truck, but glancing down I realize we're going nearly sixty miles an hour on a neighborhood street. Adrenaline rushes through me as I try to make quick decisions, knowing Lisa and Allie are in danger and I'm the only one who knows.

"Uh, yes, someone has been abducted," I reply, not recognizing my own voice. It sounds distant and erratic, kind of like my heart, which is now lodged in my throat. "A black truck, a Ford, I think, took a woman and her child. He forced them into the vehicle and is now driving dangerously down Smith. We're approaching Seventh Street," I tell her, not wanting to run the stop sign, but afraid to lose sight of the truck. "Please send someone."

She instructs me to not put myself in danger, but says that if I can get the license plate number it would be helpful. When I see him blow through another stop sign, I realize there's no way I'll be able to catch him. Then he makes another turn, and the back end fishtails.

For a split second, I pray for some sort of collision to slow him down. As long as Lisa and Allie don't get hurt. It would be better than him getting away with them.

"Ma'am," the dispatcher says, getting my attention.

"I'm sorry," I tell her, my own tires screeching as I make the same turn. When I do, the black truck is nowhere to be found. Gone. Like it just disappeared without a trace.

Still driving fast, I look in every parking lot and side street. Now that I'm on one of the main roads, the traffic is thicker, and more people are out and about. It would be hard for him to continue driving the way he was without being noticed, so I hope he's sitting somewhere and I'll see them.

"I'm dispatching the police to the area," she says. "If you see the truck again, please call back, but don't put yourself in harm's way."

I would do that. For Lisa and Allie, I would.

But I don't get the chance, because after an hour of driving around Maryville, I don't see the truck anywhere. Eventually, I go to the shelter, where Helen is waiting with a worried expression.

"Lisa and Allie—"

"Have you seen them?" I ask, hope beginning to build in my chest, filling the space left when I lost the truck. "Are they here?"

"No," Helen says, confusion replacing the worry. "Did you see them?"

Feeling my last drop of hope leak out, I lean back on my car and lower my chin to my chest, fighting back the emotions. As the frustration takes over, I let out a growl, turning to kick the tire on my car.

Stupid car.

Stupid, old, slow car.

"I saw them this morning on my way here. They were walking down First Street. They were a few blocks ahead of me when I spotted them. I was sitting at a stop sign when a black truck pulled up and a guy forced them inside. It happened so fast . . . I tried to follow them, but couldn't . . . and I called the police . . ."

My words trail off as Helen's arm comes up to wrap around my shoulder, turning me to her.

"We'll find them," she says, her business mode on in full-force.

"Let's go inside and I'll make a few more calls. They couldn't have gotten too far."

I shake my head. "I've searched this whole city over. Twice. You don't understand. They're just . . . gone. I should've gone faster, been quicker—"

"It's not your fault." She's now holding both of my shoulders firmly in her grasp and leveling me with her steel-grey eyes. "Come inside. Let's make some calls and figure this out."

As we walk into the shelter, I feel an immediate loss as I look around the dining area and see two empty seats where Lisa and Allie have been sitting. It's wrong. They should be here. "Why did they leave?" I ask Helen as we continue past the dining room onto the hallway that leads to our offices.

"She didn't say," Helen says with a heavy sigh. "I didn't even know they'd left until I checked the log. But seeing as she'd logged out, I'm guessing she had every intention of logging back in." Grabbing said log, she points to the signature and time.

"It doesn't make sense. Where would they be going this early in the morning?"

Helen takes a seat at her desk, picking up the phone. "Your guess is as good as mine," she says, dialing a number. She's quiet for a second as the phone rings. Faintly, I can hear a man's voice answer on the other end.

"Yes, this is Helen Harrison from the women's shelter," she begins, glancing up at me and then back down at the papers in front of her. "I'd like to follow up on a call one of my volunteers made this morning about one of our tenants being abducted."

She listens, and I wait.

The frown that forms isn't a good sign and I watch as Helen's back stiffens. "She witnessed it. That should be enough information to go off of. And there is a child involved! I also have the log here in front of me where she signed out. I don't think she would've done that if she didn't plan on coming back. I'd like this to be taken seriously. She came to us for refuge—that should be evidence enough that foul play is involved here."

At some point, the person on the other end tells Helen he'll send a police officer to fill out a report and get a case opened. Typically, that wouldn't happen until a person has been gone for twenty-four hours, but since a child is involved and I witnessed it happen, an Amber Alert was immediately issued.

An hour or so later, the reports have been filed. Every detail we know about Lisa and Allie Sanchez has been written down. The description of the truck is now in the hands of every patrol officer in the state.

"These types of cases are often difficult to crack. If you'd been able to get a license plate number, we'd have more to go off of. But since the only information we have is what you *think* is a black Ford pickup," he says, giving me a look. "Our best hope is he gets pulled over for a traffic violation."

A missing person report will go out to other police departments in the area. Then, we have a chance of Lisa or Allie being spotted, if and when they stop. That is, unless whoever took them doesn't want them to be found. Remote locations are a dime a dozen in Tennessee.

When the officer leaves, Helen and I both sit in her office in complete silence, staring at the white walls.

I wonder if she feels as helpless as I do?

"You should go home before it gets dark." It's the first thing either of us has said in a while and the raspiness in her voice shows it. She stands and gathers her trusty clipboard. "I'll call you if I hear anything."

For some reason, I don't argue with her. Instead, I grab my phone and my bag and follow her out into the hallway. "Do you think we'll find them?"

She stops, but doesn't turn to face me. "I hope we do."

I guess that's as good as it gets at this point. I swallow down the lump in my throat.

"Frankie," she says before I walk out the door. "Are you okay?"

I nod, biting down on my lip as I take a step outside. "Yeah, I'm fine."

"You're going straight home, right?" she asks, a hint of nervousness in her tone.

Again, I nod.

"Please call me when you get there, and I'll call you when I hear anything."

"Okay." Tuning, I give her a small smile, hoping it's reassuring enough to set her mind at ease. Don't get me wrong, I did think about driving around looking for the black truck, but I'm smart enough to know it's like looking for a needle in a haystack.

If I could think of anything else to do to help them, I would, but I can't.

On the drive to Green Valley, I begin to finally let the emotions I've tamped down all day rise to the surface. Being a person who doesn't allow herself to feel very often, I'm caught off guard by the immense sadness and guilt that washes over me.

I should've done more.

I wish I would've been there sooner . . . driven faster . . . been more observant.

Everything about the two of them reminds me of me and my mother and I can't get past that.

As I pass the Piggly Wiggly, my thoughts turn to Gunnar, and I know where I want to go.

Pulling up outside the studio I've only ever driven past, I put my car in park and immediately see the person I'm looking for, who I need. Gunnar is inside and I watch as he punches a bag hanging from the ceiling.

I expect the familiar burning in the pit of my stomach, and there is a burning inside me—but it has nothing to do with violence.

For a brief moment, I wonder what I'm doing here. Gunnar is obviously busy and might not want me here, but then I quickly dismiss that. If know anything at all, it's that Gunnar wants me.

He's told me.

But better yet, he's shown me.

I trust him.

CHAPTER 17

GUNNAR

I should be exhausted. I've completed two rounds of training, did my usual lifting routine, and sparred with a few guys from the gym. But instead of taking the rest of the evening off like I know I should, I'm still here punching the bags. It's as though I can't burn off enough energy, and if I sit still for too long, I get antsy.

It would be easy to say I'm sexually frustrated—and that's certainly part of the problem—but it's more than that. I still don't know where I stand with Frankie or how she feels about me, and I'm no closer to figuring out her connection with the Iron Wraiths than I was a week ago. I worry about her safety until my stomach hurts, even though I know she's been dealing with them for longer than I've been in Green Valley. And to make matters worse, I walked in on Tempest and Cage going at it in the bathroom this morning. Most body parts were covered, thank God, but I still saw and heard way more than I needed to.

Maybe I just need a beer or a night out on the town. I'd fly back to Dallas for a weekend, but that'd mean leaving Frankie and that's absolutely out of the question. Maybe I can talk her into going to Dallas with me once the charity event is over. To be able to take her away and go anywhere—just the two of us, where we can just be *us* without any responsibilities for a day or two—sounds incredible.

I make a mental note to add that to my mile-long to-do list.

Feeling much calmer than I was a few minutes ago, I decide to stop for the day. I remove my gloves and towel off as best I can, only pausing to take a few large swigs from my water bottle. When I bend down to grab my bag from a nearby bench, movement from the other side of the large window catches my eye.

Frankie.

Frankie has never been here before, not to my knowledge, and she looks like she's gonna bolt any second now. Without thinking or putting on my shirt, I run over to the door and push it open.

"Hey, are you okay? What's going on?"

Her face is an open book at the moment, which is so uncharacteristic of her that it throws me for a second. She looks sad and tired, but also a bit skittish. As I step out onto the sidewalk, I'm fighting against every instinct within me. I want to reach out and wrap her in my arms, to provide protection from whatever is hurting her.

When her eyes find mine, they're red-rimmed and glassy. I can tell she's been crying and it kills me. "Hey," I say, finally extending my hand toward her like you would a hurt animal—letting her know I'm here and I mean no harm. "Frankie . . . I'm right here. Tell me what's wrong. What happened?"

She looks away and then back to me, a desperation in her expression I've never seen before.

"I need you."

Three words. Three simple words that make me want to soar. I don't make her repeat them because, even though they came out in a whisper, I heard them loud and clear. I close the distance between us and take her hand. Whatever is going on, I'll handle it, but the important thing is she's here. She came to me.

"Come on, I'll drive you home. You can leave your car here. Grab what you need from it."

She doesn't argue or question me, which means she's still in some kind of state of shock or something and I say a quick prayer, thanking God she made it to the gym safely. It's obvious she should not be driving right now.

When she's buckled up in the cab of the truck, I hop in the driver's seat and start the engine. Frankie immediately relaxes into the leather seat and closes her eyes. I have to take a few cleansing breaths before I'm able to start driving because my adrenaline has kicked into overdrive. I'm so relieved she came to me, though, and I let that feeling settle into my bones while I drive us to Frankie's house.

Once we're there, Frankie seems more like herself as she opens her front door and motions for me to follow her inside. She's still not talking, but I gladly do what she wants because she's in control right now.

When I'm inside, she locks the door behind me and grabs my hand, leading me straight to her bedroom. Never breaking eye contact, Frankie kicks off her shoes before sliding her jeans over her hips and down her legs. She then does some kind of move from that old Flashdance movie and manages to pull her bra through the sleeve of her shirt, tossing it on top of her jeans. I'm still standing in front of her, not knowing what I'm supposed to do next, when she crawls into her bed and gets under the covers.

"Will you hold me while I sleep?" Her voice is quiet—but the blood rushing through my eardrums is not. This right here is probably the most intimate I've ever been with a woman and my clothes are still on.

Please, God, don't let me fuck this up.

I strip down to my boxers, ignoring the fact I haven't showered, and follow her into bed.

At this point, I'd do anything she asks.

Fly to the moon.

Run with the bulls in Spain.

Holding her while she sleeps would be my honor.

Once I'm under the covers, she immediately latches onto my body, as if she's afraid I'll disappear. I want to reassure her and tell her I'm here to stay for as long as she wants me, but the moment feels like it'd be ruined with words.

Instead, I wrap my arms around her and kiss the top of her head, breathing in her scent. Staring off into the darkness of her bedroom, my mind wanders, making up scenarios and trying not to jump to conclusions. With every soft breath she takes, I remind myself she's here, and she's whole, and that's all that matters.

Eventually, I fall asleep too, the exhaustion from my day catching up with me.

When I feel the bed dip, I wake with a start. Remembering where I am takes me a moment, but then I see Frankie's beautiful face. Even in the dark, I can tell she's watching me.

"I've been dreaming of this for a while now." Her words are hushed and soft.

"Dreaming of what, exactly?"

"You holding me like this," she says, shifting so her chin is resting on my chest. "I've been wondering what it feels like to fall asleep in your arms and now I know."

I chuckle quietly, afraid to disrupt the bubble we're in. "What's the verdict?"

"It was even better than I imagined." She smiles before leaning down and placing a kiss on my chest. It's such a simple action, but it causes my heart to skip a beat all the same. "I've had other kinds of dreams about you, too."

These words cause a completely different reaction below my waist.

"You gonna tell me about those, too?" I ask, wanting more, but not wanting to push.

"I'd rather show you."

Oh, hell, yeah.

Frankie's mouth is on mine before I can register what's happening, but I quickly catch on and latch onto her ass, pulling her further up my body. The kiss isn't frantic, like I feel; it's slow and meaningful. If ever a kiss could change the course of my life, this one is it.

Placing her hands on my chest, she pushes up, breaking the kiss and straddling my waist, just like she did the other night in my truck. I'm hopeful things will end differently this time.

"There's something I need to tell you first," she says swallowing, and I'm afraid this is it, the breaking point where she gets scared and shuts me out. "I have scars. On my back." Her hand drifts to where I'm assuming said scars are, and again, I try not to jump to any conclusions. She's sharing a part of herself, something that obviously bothers her, and I refuse to make her feel bad about it. "And here," she says, pointing to her thigh. "And here." Her hand goes up to her chest and I cover it with my own.

"I don't care about any of that." I tell her, my voice rough. "Scars or no scars, I want you."

When she takes off her top and tosses it to the floor, she takes my breath right along with it.

She's baring not only her body to me, but her soul.

For a moment, I soak her in, devouring every inch of her I can see in the dim light. I want to tattoo this moment on my skin . . . in my heart . . . make it a permanent piece of me.

"You're so fucking beautiful." My voice is strained, tense from the pounding in my chest, but I mean what I say. She is, without a doubt, the most beautiful person I've ever known—mind, body, and soul. And tonight, I'm making her mine.

Sitting up, I pull her closer to me—her heat radiating to my cock —and kiss her, claiming her, begging her to be mine. I nip the delicate skin of her jaw, making my way down her throat and across her chest. When she arches her back, I suck one of her nipples into my mouth, rolling my tongue around the sensitive peak. Moving from one breast to the other and back, I continue to devour her until she's gasping and writhing in my arms.

"I need to know what you want," I breathe against her skin, slipping two fingers beneath the elastic band of her panties. I'm dying to go further—feel more, take more—but I need to know *this* is what she wants. "I want you, Frankie. Please tell me you want me too."

"Make love to me," she whispers, and although it's quiet and a bit hesitant, there's a sureness in her tone that lets me know she's ready. "Please."

Her choice of words does something funny to my insides, but I push that to the side. I'm not letting my brain get in the way of this moment. I'm finally about to be inside Frankie and she could be speaking Klingon right now and I wouldn't really care.

Finally, I slip my hand further inside her panties and my fingers are met with the most exquisite warmth and slickness. The fact that she's wet and ready for me is enough to make me come, but when I push a single finger inside her pussy and she bucks against my straining cock, I'm a goner.

This time, I'm the one who gasps, thrusting against her instinctively, ready for every barrier between us to disappear.

"Lift up," I instruct, pulling her panties down her legs and tossing them to the side. I discard my boxers as quickly as I can. When we're both naked, I roll us onto our sides. There's no power struggle here, there's only the most intense connection I've ever felt in my life. It's tangible. And feelings, so many fucking feelings I can't even acknowledge right now, but they're there.

Grabbing her calf, I can't help but relish in the way her skin feels beneath mine. So fucking good. She's everything. Everything I wanted, everything I hoped she'd be, and so much more.

Just as I'm getting ready to slip inside her and give us both what we need, what we want, I freeze. "Condom?" I ask, my heart beating wildly in my chest and my breaths already coming out labored from pure desire. "I didn't bring one."

"I'm on the pill," she says, her chest rising and falling with each breath. "It's fine. Please."

Without another word, I lift her leg just enough to make room between her luscious thighs, then enter her completely in one swift thrust. She cries out, grabbing onto my shoulders and pulling me closer.

"Fuuuuck," I groan when she clenches around me. "You feel so good, Frankie. So fucking good."

"God, yes," she moans. "So good."

I increase my pace, thrusting harder and harder until I know we're both close.

"Look at me," I command.

When her hooded eyes find mine, I lean forward and capture her lips, slowing my pace to stave off my orgasm and enjoy this moment with her. "Now, look at where we're joined." She does, and I follow her gaze, watching as I pump inside her.

"This is us," I pant, my speed increasing with the need building. "You. Me. Us."

My breaths are choppy as I continue, wanting her to know she's mine and I'm hers.

She groans, her head lolling back as my hands grip her hips tighter.

"Tell me, Frankie. Tell me you feel this."

I probably sound crazy to her. Hell, I sound a little crazy to myself, but I'm desperate for her to realize how different this feels, how special this moment is, how special she is. More than anything, I need her to be on the same page.

"Fuck, yes," she breathes, bringing those gorgeous eyes back to mine. "I feel it, Gunnar. You. Me. Everything."

Her words spur me on, causing my hips to push harder. This position allows me to be deep inside her while hitting just the right spot for some delicious friction. Soon, we're both chasing our release.

A few minutes later, we come together, our bodies slick with sweat, spasming and pulsing as one until we're completely spent.

CHAPTER 18

FRANKIE

$\mathcal{I}$ wake with a start, the same dream I've been having for the past few weeks interrupting what might possibly have been the best sleep I've had in ages. When I try to sit up, a strong arm pulls me back against an even stronger chest.

Gunnar Erickson is in my bed.

We had sex.

The best sex I've ever had.

Giving in to his efforts, I sink back in the bed and close my eyes, breathing him in while I try to calm the erratic beating of my heart, partly due to the memories flooding back from the middle of the night and partly due to the dream I just had.

His mouth finds my neck, sending chills up and down my spine.

"It's Saturday," he announces, but I already knew that.

I'm suddenly very aware of everything, actually. All five senses are firing on all cylinders. His musky, manly scent, with hints of his cologne, permeate my small bedroom. And us—the two of us mingle together for an erotic combination. There are hints of his taste lingering on my tongue. All I hear are his husky breaths and soft moans as he becomes fully awake. And I feel him—his strong arms and lips, as well as his erection at my back. I see him everywhere. Even when my eyes are closed, I still see him. Visions of last night come surging back with vivid images of his muscles flexing as he plunged inside me.

I can still feel it—him. There's a delicious ache between my legs.

He's everywhere, consuming every part of me—mind, body, and soul.

And as wonderful as he is, I'm having trouble processing it all, compartmentalizing it—him. I was telling the truth when I told him he doesn't fit into any one compartment. He takes over; fills in empty spaces. I love it, yet it scares the shit out of me.

How can I let one person infiltrate me so completely?

It seems reckless.

Dangerous.

Glancing over at the clock, I see it's only a quarter until six. That might seem early to most people, but I'm up before six on a regular basis. If it's not for work, then it's for volunteering. On Saturdays, I set up at the farmer's market. Except I didn't make it to my mother's this week, so I don't have much to sell, not unless I make an impromptu trip out there.

"I have to go," I blurt, not loudly, but abruptly, causing Gunnar to tighten his grip. "To my mother's," I add, trying to soften the blow. "I didn't make it out there on Thursday and I have nothing to sell this morning at the farmer's market. Besides that, I need to check on her and this is my only opportunity. I have groceries for her."

My explanation is a bit of a ramble, and when I roll over to face Gunnar I see the concern on his face. "Want me to drive out there with you?"

"Don't you need to train?"

His eyes roam my face before trailing down, settling on the base of my neck. When he reaches out to softly trace one of my faint scars, his brows furrow and I tense at his scrutiny, feeling the need to cover up. Last night, in the dark, as I was being swept away in the intense passion, I wanted him to see me, all of me. But this morning, in the light of day, I'm not so sure.

"I've never shown anyone," I start, drawing the sheet up to my chin.

Gunnar doesn't allow it. He gently pulls it back down. "Thank you for showing me. Thank you for . . . everything," he says, his voice thick as he swallows, those sea-glass eyes coming back to mine. "Don't ever feel like you need to hide from me, Frankie. I want to see every scar, know every secret."

"Why the frown?" I ask, reaching up to smooth out the skin between his brows with my thumb.

"It's not the scars." Leaning forward, he places a kiss on the puckered skin. "It's whatever caused them. I want to take it all away, avenge you, make all your wrongs right."

That admission makes me equally warm and cold at the same time. If I knew the wrongs that needed to be made right, it might not make me so anxious. But I don't know, so how can I tell Gunnar? If I told him what little bit my mind has allowed me to see, it would sound crazy, possibly the overactive imagination of a scared little girl.

I have no way of knowing what is true and what is make-believe.

All the more reason I have to go see my mother—she owes me some answers.

Sliding out from under Gunnar's arm, I get a grunt of disapproval. "Don't feel like you have to get up. I know it's early, but if I don't get out there now, I have no chance of making it back before the farmer's market."

"It's okay," Gunnar says, a ring of disappointment in his tone. Climbing out of bed to stand in front of me, he takes me by my hips and turns me to face him. "As long as you don't shut me out, I'm good with anything."

I fight back a small smile, because even though we've only known each other for a short time, he already knows me. He reads me . . . sees me, even through the walls I know I have up. I've worked hard on those walls and they've served me well, but when it comes to Gunnar, they're useless.

He makes me feel safe.

He makes me feel everything.

I don't need walls when he's around.

"I won't," I promise. Even though I'm not one hundred percent certain I can keep it, I want to.

Claiming my mouth, he steals my breath as he swipes his tongue across mine, making my belly tighten with need. When I wrap my arms around his neck, our bodies collide and I relish in the way his skin feels against mine.

More, I want more, but I also need a chance to think and wrap my mind around this influx of emotions. Pulling back and breaking the kiss, I immediately regret it, but it's what I need. When he's kissing me, touching me, I forget everything else.

He's stealing more than my breath; he's stealing my heart.

"Meet me at the farmer's market?" I ask, lacing my fingers with his. I hope he hears the unspoken words between that question: *this isn't over. I'm not running. I just need a minute to let my brain catch up with my heart.*

"Sure," he says, averting his eyes. "Maybe I could cook you dinner later. If you want."

There's the vulnerability that somehow looks so damn sexy on him. I can't resist it—or him—when he exposes himself like that. "I'd love that."

He rewards me with a wicked smile that goes straight to my core.

Fifteen minutes later, we're walking out my front door. While I was showering in my bathroom, Gunnar used the guest bathroom. Somehow, we moved around each other in perfect cadence, like two people who'd been existing in the same space for a long time. It was weird, yet comfortable.

When we pull up in front of the studio, the windows inside are dark and my car is the only one on this side of the street. Gunnar parks behind it and turns off the engine. We both sit in silence for a few moments and then his hand reaches for mine.

"Promise me if you want to talk, you'll talk to me?" he asks, his gaze meeting mine, eyes pleading. "And I promise I'm not going to push. But I'm here for you, whenever, however, whatever you need."

"Okay."

"Want to tell me about yesterday?" His hand gives mine a gentle squeeze of reassurance as I realize I never told him why I was upset or what sent me to the studio. I feel bad. I owed him that much, but when we got to my house, all I could think about was being close to him and letting him take away the day.

"A mother and daughter from the shelter were abducted yesterday," I tell him, glancing at my phone lying in my lap. There's nothing on it—no missed call from Helen. "I saw it happen."

He stills his hand. "I'm sorry . . .I—"

"Why would you be? It's not your fault," I tell him, not realizing I'm snapping at him until it's already out of my mouth. Biting down on my cheek, I wince. I hate that about myself. The way I can just turn on someone. It's a coping mechanism, I know that, but it's the worst and it always makes me feel shitty when it happens, and yet, I seem to have no control over it.

When he shifts in his seat, I wait for his departure, thinking he'll leave me sitting here like he left me standing at the farmer's market the last time I lashed out at him. "I'm sorry." Turning toward him, this time I'm the one to reach out to him. "That was rude. You were just being compassionate. I don't know why I do that."

"You do it to protect yourself," he says matter-of-factly. "Maybe a part of you wants to drive me away because it's easier for you to deal with your emotions when you're alone."

I fight back a smile. "Are you sure you didn't go to college to be a psychologist?"

"No." He shakes his head, giving me a small smile. "But I'm good at reading people. My mom says it's a gift. A sixth sense, if you will."

I nod, admiring Gunnar in the early morning light, soaking him in. He really is beautiful, inside and out. He deserves my trust and honesty. I want to give it to him, but it's going to take time. "They remind me of my mother and me," I admit, starting with this small piece of myself. "The mother and child—Lisa and Allie. When I see them together, it's like I'm transported back to when I was at the shelter."

Gunnar's head cocks to one side, but he stays quiet, patiently waiting for more.

"My mother sought shelter there. I was seven. And my first memory was from the day we checked in. Helen gave me a teddy bear. Everything before that is dark and murky. I can't remember anything before that day." I want to add, "except for screaming and pain," but I can't. Not yet.

Baby steps.

He nods his head, processing the information. Thankfully, there's no judgment on his face, or worse, pity. He just accepts it and asks, "What about Lisa and Allie? What happened?"

I give him a brief summary of yesterday, starting with me turning off the main road and seeing them walking, and ending with the police officer coming to take the official report.

"I felt helpless and all I could think about was getting to you."

Instead of saying anything, he draws me to him, enveloping me in his arms. "Thank you," he whispers, his voice rough at my ear, yet gentle all the same. "For trusting me with this. And for coming to me."

He keeps me safe in his embrace for a few long moments. I close my eyes and breathe him in, clinging to his t-shirt like a lifeline. We soak each other in, him taking part of my burden and me taking part of his strength. "Is there anything I can do to help?" he asks, pulling back enough that we're nose to nose.

I shake my head. "I don't even know what I'm supposed to do." His lips brush mine, not in a needy kiss, but a soft reminder—*I'm here . . . it's okay.* "The officer who took the report said cases like this are unpredictable, and since I didn't get a tag number, there's not a lot to go off of, except her ex, who we don't have much information about."

Gunnar grunts his disapproval. "That's not your fault."

"I know," I say with a sigh, leaning back and letting my eyes travel outside of the truck. The sun is fully up, and I know I'm limited for time if I'm going to make it back for the farmer's market. "I should go."

"You sure you don't want to come in for a cup of coffee?" he asks. "Or we could go across the street to the bakery and make Tempest feed us muffins."

Smiling, I bring my eyes back to him and roam his face, categorizing every perfect imperfection: the scar that's healing nicely, and another small one under the opposite eye. They remind me of my own, some more noticeable than others. "Another time?" I ask, hoping I can have a rain check.

"You got it."

There's a promise there, like he's planning on holding me to it, and I hope he does.

A few minutes later, I'm sliding into the driver's seat of my car and waving at Gunnar who's still standing on the sidewalk looking a little forlorn, and I'm forced to smile. He makes me smile. I give him one last wave and pull away from the curb, slowly, watching him in my rearview mirror.

Never, in my wildest dreams—mostly because I never allowed myself to have dreams, wild or otherwise—did I ever imagine meeting someone like Gunnar Erickson.

He's an anomaly. A divergence from the path my life was on.

I can already tell that even if he realizes I'm more work than I'm worth, or I decide he's just too much for me to handle, my life will be separated into two parts: B.G.E. and A.G.E.

Before Gunnar Erickson pushed his way past my walls, and after.

As I make my way out of town, past the Piggly Wiggly and then onto the Parkway, I let my mind wander to what it would be like to completely give myself over to the myriad of feelings and emotions coursing through my body and dominating my brain. It's so great a departure from my normal compartmentalizing that it scares me, so I turn my attention to the trees instead.

Tennessee is beautiful.

The drive to my mother's cabin is one of my favorites. It's off the beaten path, one of her favorite parts about it. If you don't know what you're looking for, you'll miss it. She drove me out here a couple of times when I was little. Once, for an entire week. I remember eating peanut butter sandwiches and reading books by candlelight. I was maybe eight or nine. The nights were cold, but we had sleeping bags and she made me wear her oversized sweater that smelled like her—earthy and woodsy with hints of floral.

It's a good memory.

But now as an adult, I realize it might not have been exactly as I remember it. When you're a child, you easily believe what adults tell you. Whoever you trust most in life is your beacon, directing you in the right path. But that's a lot of responsibility and it's easily abused, used to direct a child's eyes to the apple in an effort to avoid the snake.

I feel like that's what my mother did.

She redirected my attention to see what she wanted me to see, to hide the ugly truth. But today, I need her to give me more. At twenty-five years old, I deserve to know the truth.

Driving up the wooded path, I eventually come to the small cabin.

It looks a bit fairytale-ish in the early morning light. The entire front is almost entirely covered in ivy and my mother has plants everywhere—pots and beds and hanging baskets. What doesn't fit in her greenhouse out back, she has scattered around the yard. Pausing for a moment in my car before getting out, I appreciate the simplistic beauty.

"Francis?" my mother calls from the porch, a confused and worried expression on her face.

Opening the car door, I step out and grab the bag of groceries that have been in my car since Tuesday night—boxed milk, her favorite cookies, pectin for making jam, and a bag of flour. You know, the basics for hermits. "Hi, Mom."

"Is everything okay?"

She's always worried when things are out of order or off-kilter.

That's probably where I get my rigid schedule from. Unlike her, I can adapt when I need to, but she's a lot less malleable.

"Everything is fine," I assure her, walking up to the front step of the small porch. "I missed my visit on Thursday and didn't get to bring you the things you asked for from the store."

"Oh," she says, relaxing a little as she wipes her hands on a tattered apron. "Well, in that case, it's good to see you."

Taking a second to look her over, making sure she's taking care of herself, I reply, "I also thought I'd get whatever you have to sell at the farmer's market. If I hurry, I can make it back into town before everything gets going."

She smiles, a genuine, full smile. "I found another batch of dandelion jelly," she announces, like she's found a hidden treasure. I'll give it to her, the dandelion jelly is good. It's so sweet and tastes like honey, but she gets a little overly-excited about her jams and jellies.

"That sold well," I tell her, following her around to the back of the cabin. "Oh, here's your money from last week." Handing her the folded bills, she takes them and peels off the top twenty, just like always, and hands it to me.

I've told her time and time again she doesn't have to pay me, but she insists. Usually, I put it back into her grocery money, which she also tries to pay me for, but I never give her the real total. If she ever decides to get off this piece of property and go to the store for herself, she'd be in for a serious case of sticker shock.

"I also have a few jars of honey," she says, holding them up to show me. "Make sure you get top dollar for this—no haggling."

Nodding, I hold out my arms and let her begin to fill them with her goods. "I wanted to ask you something," I say, figuring now was as good a time as any.

"What's that?" she asks, standing up and brushing her wild blonde hair out of her face. I almost hate disrupting the soft smile she's wearing, but I can't help it. I need answers.

"We weren't in a car wreck, were we?" That's always been her story, whenever I asked about the scars. When I was younger and started noticing the marks on my skin, she made up an elaborate story about how we were riding in a car with a friend of hers and a deer ran across the road, sending the vehicle into a tailspin. There was glass and that's how she explained away the scars.

She blinks her eyes a few times. It's her tell when she's covering the truth, so I press.

"I've been having these dreams," I start, swallowing down the thickness in my throat from the flashes of memory, or what I think are memories. "I'm screaming. Well, not me now, but a younger me. I know it's me," I say, sitting the jars of honey on the grass at my feet. "I feel it right here."

My hand goes to the space right under my sternum.

"And then," I continue. "I started seeing something else . . ." Trailing off, I'm afraid to mention this last part. It's a new development, and it involves her. It's more than the phantom pain I feel when the younger Frankie screams in my dreams; this part is worse. "You're standing in front of me and there's a man . . . and . . . and he hits you . . ." *Every time, over and over*. I don't continue because it's too painful to repeat; from the look on her face, it's painful to hear.

When she turns her back to me, facing the greenhouse, my insides grow cold.

I think, deep down, I was hoping she'd tell me it's a horrible dream—feeding me the lies she's been telling me my whole life. But she doesn't. For the first time, she breaks character. No longer is she the delusional mother who lives in the woods.

As she turns back around to face me, she's a different person—scared, hiding a painful past—and I suddenly feel guilty for making her relive even a small part of it.

"Was that my father?" I ask, needing to go ahead and open the wound.

Sometimes, when an injury doesn't heal properly, the only thing you can do is cut it open, clean out the infection, and start over.

Her solemn nod is all I get. Without another word, she hands me a crate loaded down with jars and walks away. Before I can even get around to the front, she's inside with the door shut.

I could push for more, but this is the most honest she's been with me in eighteen years. So, I take what she's given, bits of the truth and her jars, and climb back in my car.

When I make my way back to town, I turn off the main road and instinctively glance in my rearview mirror, noticing a bike trailing me. Initially, my heart jumps into my throat, wondering how long it's been following me, but assure myself I would've seen him if he'd been there long.

Regardless, I had to look both ways before getting back on the Parkway. I would've seen him then, which means he had to have started following me after that. So, I take comfort in knowing he didn't see where I'd been.

It's not until I pull off at an abandoned gas station that I'm even sure it's an Iron Wraith. But when the bike follows me, I know. However, I don't recognize the man who pulls up behind my car. He's older than the ones who usually track me down. His leather cut is a bit more worn. And there's a difference in his gait as he approaches the car. It's not demanding or threatening, and for some reason, that puts me on edge. Because like my mother, I always like to know what to expect, and this isn't it.

"Frankie," he says with a nod as he comes into my line of sight. I'd already rolled my window down, ready to get this over with. I don't care what they want today; I'm not going with him. My emotions are at the surface as it is and I'm not interested in having them boil over.

Turning to look at him, I squint against the morning sun. "Do I know you?" I ask, an edge to my voice.

He chuckles, shaking his head as he stands up straight and looks out toward the road. "You don't want to, but I know you."

The way he says it has the hairs on my arms standing to attention. It sounds lethal and brooks no argument. Then he adds, "I know your mama, too."

This has me turning in my seat and reaching for the door handle. I don't know what I'm planning on doing when I get out of my car,

147

but I feel the need to stand up to him and find out exactly how he knows my mother.

Could *he* be my father?

"Stay in the fucking car," he growls. His tone isn't as aggressive as his words. He sounds more put out that he's standing here talking to me than anything. "And before you ask, no, I'm not your daddy."

My chest deflates as I lean back against the seat. I don't know if I'm relieved or disappointed with that bit of information. Maybe a little of both. I'm exhausted for sure, and ready for this whole thing to be over with, but I don't know how to end it without the truth. "Who is?"

Again, he shakes his head and paces beside my car, kicking up rocks as he goes. "You don't really want to know. You think you do —but you don't. Won't matter anyhow."

"What's that supposed to mean?" I ask, my voice rising with the anger. "I'm sick and tired of the bullshit and lies." Hitting the steering wheel with the palms of my hands, I let out a growl of frustration. "I don't want to do it anymore—patch up your stupid club members. I'm done."

"That's good, because it's over." He stops, hands on his hips, exposing what looks like the butt of a gun in the waistband of his jeans. I swallow, feeling the familiar burning sensation in the pit of my stomach. *What does he plan on doing with that?*

He follows my line of sight and smirks, chuckling lowly. "Don't worry, sweetheart, not planning on using that today. Not right now, anyway."

"What's over?" I ask, going back to his statement.

"You're no longer the doctor on call," he says. "No one will come looking for you, but you have to promise me one thing."

It's over.

How will I get my answers?

How will I ever know who my father is?

How will I know the missing pieces?

"What?" I finally ask, feeling more tired than I have in a long time.

"Drop it. Don't come snooping around the Dragon. I don't want to see you anywhere near the compound."

"And if I do?" I ask, feeling brave and out of fucks to give.

He doesn't give me a verbal answer. He just pulls his leather vest back to expose the gun, the steel gleaming in the sunlight.

CHAPTER 19

GUNNAR

"So, you're coming to the benefit?" I ask, kissing the top of Frankie's head, breathing her in. I make it a point not to call it a fight. After the first few times I brought it up and she winced at the term, I changed my tactic. If she keeps the word "benefit" in mind, remembering it's for the shelter, it helps her *compartmentalize*, as she calls it.

I'm all for whatever makes her comfortable.

"I said I'd be there," she says, turning into my side and wrapping her arms around my torso. "I'll be there."

Over the past week, since our first night together, Frankie's been . . . different.

When she met me at the farmer's market after visiting her mom last Saturday, I could tell something happened. I said I wasn't going to pry, so I'm not. It's taking every ounce of self-discipline that's been drilled into me over the years, but somehow I've refrained.

The only thing she told me was that her mother shared something about her past and she's processing. As long as that doesn't include pushing me away again, I'm good with it.

We've been good and found a rhythm. Kind of like in a fight, when two opponents dance around each other—one goes left as the other goes right. If I see I'm encroaching on her personal space and it's making her uncomfortable, I pull back. When she realizes she's putting up her walls, she gives in a little.

On the days she works her shifts at the hospital, I've been doubling up on training and helping Cage and Vali with the preparations for the fight. Vali made it to town a few days ago and we've been going nonstop ever since. So, tonight, when Frankie got off her last twelve-hour shift for the week, I met her at her house.

The make-out session started in the driveway, both of us needing the other. With her legs wrapped around me, I dug her key out of her bag and let us in, not even making it to her bedroom before I was inside her.

Just thinking about it has me pulling her onto my chest, her leg hitching over my hip. "I thought you were tired," she whispers in a husky tone that's quickly become my favorite sound. Well, second to Frankie laughing. I'll take that all day, every day. But this husky, needy tone she has when it's just the two of us in bed together feels like it belongs to me. I'm the only one who gets to hear it. I'm the cause of it. And I fucking love it.

"Never too tired for you," I tell her. "I want you. Always."

Her eyes lock with mine as her hands come up to frame my face. I can see there are words right on the tip of her tongue, hanging in the air between us. But instead of saying them, she presses her lips to mine. At first, it's soft and slow, less a kiss and more a way to keep herself from saying something she's not ready to say.

After a few moments, she inhales deeply before scraping her teeth against my bottom lip, sending chills down my spine. The sensation goes straight to my dick, causing me to buck against her and grabbing her hips to gain friction as I open my mouth to give her access.

In that moment, everything goes from patient to desperate. Her hands move from my face to my chest as she uses me for leverage, rolling her hot center against my hardening dick. There's only a thin layer of clothing between us—her panties and my boxers. Thanking God and every entity listening for Frankie being on birth control, I slip my hand between us, pulling the silky fabric to the side and plunging two fingers into her.

"Ahhh," she cries out, breaking the kiss. Her head falls back and her mouth opens, exposing her delicate neck. Grazing my lips from her collarbone to the sensitive spot behind her ear, I groan. "Come for me, Frankie. Let me hear you."

BC

A loud whimper wakes me and I immediately roll toward Frankie, searching her face in the dark. Her eyes are still closed so I assume she's still asleep, but whatever she's dreaming about is causing her obvious distress. Pulling her back against my chest, I wrap my arms protectively around her, seeing if my proximity can soothe the bad dream and lull her back into the peaceful sleep she was in when I'd finally dozed off.

Glancing at the clock on the nightstand, I see it's only been a couple of hours since Frankie and I showered together and then promptly climbed back into bed. After two rounds of amazing sex—because every round with Frankie is amazing—we were both exhausted. Her breathing was soft and even before I even found a comfortable spot on the pillow. On my side of the bed.

I'm not sure how long it takes for a side to officially become yours, but this is my fourth night sleeping here and I claim it. It's mine. So is the beautiful girl in my arms.

When Frankie whimpers again and then clings to my arm tucked around her, I push up on my elbow to peer over at her. "Frankie?" I whisper. I don't want to startle her, but I don't like seeing her scared.

Instead of calming at my voice, she thrashes, almost elbowing me in the face.

"No," she cries out. "Don't hurt me."

"Frankie." This time I say her name louder, putting a hand up to dodge another elbow. "Frankie, wake up. You're having a bad dream."

"Don't hurt me!"

"Frankie!"

When her eyes fly open, she's disoriented and blinks rapidly, trying to see through the dark.

"I'm here," I tell her, softening my tone. "I'm here."

She relaxes a little with my reassurance and settles back on her pillow, throwing an arm over her face. Her breaths are a bit ragged as her chest rises and falls. I'm afraid to ask about her dream—not because I think she won't tell me, but because I think she will. And I'm going to want to kill whoever hurt her.

"Will it help to talk about it?" I finally ask, settling back beside her.

"No," she replies. It's small and scared and I can't allow that.

Reaching up, I remove her arm from her face and hold her stare in the dark. "You can tell me." *I can take it. I can listen and not react*, I silently tell myself. "You don't have to keep it bottled up, whatever it is."

It's quiet for a few minutes and I lean down and kiss her cheek, thinking she's not going to tell me—and once again, putting up her walls when I get too close—but then she whispers, "He hurt me."

My body wants to tense at her admission, but I force it to remain calm, not wanting to end this moment of truth-telling. "Who?"

"I don't know . . ." She pauses, hesitating for a moment. "My father, I think."

How does she not know?

"You don't remember?"

She shakes her head. "I don't remember anything. But I think . . ." She pauses, and I allow her to take all the time she needs. "I think he gave me these." When she points to the scar on her shoulder, I bite down so hard to keep from growling I think I'm going to break a tooth. Closing my eyes, I try not to imagine a man—*her father*—cutting her.

There's no way.

What father would do that to his child?

"Why?" It's all I can manage to grit out, and even then, it sounds pained—because it is. Thinking about someone hurting Frankie is

154

agonizing. My chest tightens at the thought. "Why would he do that?"

"I don't know, but I've been having dreams . . . and it's the only thing that makes sense."

No, it doesn't make any fucking sense. Not at all.

"Sometimes," I start, maintaining a quieter tone, "our dreams aren't exactly what they seem. They're more . . . symbolic."

Maybe I'm saying this for my own benefit, but I scramble to find any form of comfort for her. Shit, I'd lie, cheat, or steal, if it meant Frankie was happy.

"What would a man with a knife cutting into my skin be symbolic of?" Her voice is hollow, empty, as she sits up in bed and draws her knees to her chest.

"I don't know," I tell her, scooting over and sliding behind her. With my back against the headboard, I hold her to my chest, my arms wrapped tightly around her. Eventually, she brings her hands up and grasps my forearms.

We fall asleep like that, but this time, my sleep isn't restful and my dreams are dark and unwelcomed—violent images flashing through my mind.

When I wake again, the room isn't as dark as it was earlier, meaning it's probably close to the time when Frankie's alarm will go off. It's her morning to volunteer at the shelter and I was planning on driving to Daisy's with her for a coffee and donut.

Thankfully, Frankie stays asleep when I gently place her back on the pillow on her side of the bed. Climbing out, I stretch, groaning quietly at the slight crick in my neck. Yeah, sleeping sitting up isn't ideal, but as I look back at Frankie, something grips my heart like a vice.

I'd do anything for her.

Walking to the bathroom, I quietly shut the door and take care of business. But when I open it back up a few minutes later, Frankie is sitting on the side of the bed, looking a little better than she did when she woke from her bad dream. Or rather, nightmare. The things she described still make the hairs stand on the back of my neck.

"Hey," I say, picking my shirt up off the floor beside the bed. "How are you feeling?"

She rubs the back of her neck, groaning. "Okay. Better." When she looks up at me, her smile is apologetic and I immediately want to tell her there's nothing to be sorry for. I'm here for it—the good and the bad. There's nothing Frankie can do or say that's going to run me off.

"Don't say sorry," I tell her, squatting down so we're eye-to-eye. "There's nothing to be sorry about."

Fighting back a small smile, she shakes her head and sighs. "Can I at least buy you a donut and coffee for keeping you up all night?"

Bracing my arms on either side of her, I force my way into her personal space, my lips at her ear. "I *love* when you keep me up all night." The way her breath hitches has me smiling. I love the obvious effect I have on her and I would love nothing more than to take her back to bed, but for a completely different reason than sleeping. However, I don't want to push her, or this. I'm completely okay with taking it slow.

As I turn my head, I breathe her in and place a kiss on her temple.

BC

By the time we make it to Daisy's, Frankie is more relaxed than I've seen her in a while; maybe ever. It's like exposing that bit of ugly truth last night somehow made her feel lighter, like a small weight has been lifted.

It has left me feeling confused and frustrated, but I'll gladly carry that burden for her.

"Two jelly donuts, one maple bar, and two coffees," Frankie says, ordering for both of us. Leaning over, I can't help touching her; a small kiss to her temple, my hand on her back, twisting our fingers together as we walk to the booth. Anything to be closer to her.

Unlike our first date here, this morning is a bit more quiet, but not in an uncomfortable sense. We eat our respective donuts—one

156

jelly for her, the maple for me—and then split the second jelly. A few people I'm starting to recognize as regulars and locals walk by and give us sly smiles and glances.

Over the past few weeks, I've noticed I don't get as many stares as I did when I first showed up in Green Valley. Not for the first time, I wonder if I could see myself staying here, for more than just training.

"Whatcha thinking about?" Frankie asks, as if on cue.

Smiling, I stuff a bite of donut in my mouth to buy me a second. I don't want to talk about anything that would ruin this good vibe Frankie and I have going. There will be time for more serious conversations down the road.

"Vanilla or chocolate?" I ask, licking some jelly off my thumb.

Frankie gives me a look that says, "Are you serious?" and it's the most adorable thing I've ever seen. Chuckling, I repeat, drawing out each word, "Vanilla or chocolate?"

"That's really what you were thinking about?"

Nodding, I level her with my stare, leaning across the table to invade her space. Finally, she clears her throat and says, "Chocolate."

"Pumpkin pie or apple pie?"

She fights back a smile, but answers quicker this time, getting the gist. "Apple."

"Friends or Seinfeld?"

"Friends," she says, no questions asked.

"Morning or night?"

"Depends." Her eyes flick from the table to mine, lids a bit hooded and I notice when her tongue darts out to wet her bottom lip. It goes straight through me. The air around us seems charged.

"On what?" I ask, thankful for the table that's blocking my obscene hard-on.

"You."

Cocking my head, I pry, wanting to know everything she's thinking. "What about me?"

"If you're there, then it's my favorite."

The warmth that spreads through my chest is almost more than I can stand. To keep from rubbing at the spot over my heart, I continue with my rapid-fire questions. "Hugs or kisses?"

"Both."

I pause, letting her answer sink in and seeing the sincerity on her face, wondering how often she gets a good hug and vowing to do it every single day. And kisses, of course.

"Call or text?" I ask, remembering that I was going to ask her for her phone number. I've wanted it on several occasions, just to let her know I was thinking about her or ask her how her day was. I'm not sure if Frankie realizes it or not, but she's practically all I think about, outside of training, of course.

She shrugs. "I don't know. No one texts me, except for work. Helen always calls me."

"I'm going to text you today, and we'll revisit this question later," I tell her, reaching across for her phone and dialing my own number. When my phone rings, I hold it up and hit end. "Now I have your number."

CHAPTER 20

FRANKIE

a s I pull up to the venue, I sit in my car for a few minutes. My insides are a jittery mess, but I'm not sure why. Well, unless you consider my unreasonable fear of fighting and my aversion to it. A large portion of the human population doesn't like it, but it goes deeper with me. Part of my searching for the truth—my past, my father—is to figure out what makes me tick.

What makes Francis Delaney Reeves have nightmares about little girls screaming?

What makes her afraid?

My aversion to fighting goes beyond a feeling; it actually makes me physically ill.

But I've decided I can handle this. This is for charity and the shelter needs the money that will be raised tonight. Without it, we'd have to make cuts that would affect so many people.

Cuts.

That choice of word strikes me to my core, especially after my new onslaught of dreams. I glance down at my forearm, where one of my scars is visible for the world to see—though hardly anyone notices, except me—and mindlessly run a finger from one end of it to the other.

Helen will be here and everything will be fine.

It's not violence.

It's a sport.

But it doesn't mean people won't get hurt.

Gunnar will also be here, except he won't be with me. I've already started compartmentalizing the fight, putting him in a box with people I don't know, like I would someone who comes into my ER. It's hard, because I do know him. Actually, I feel like I know Gunnar better than anyone. He's the first person I've ever let past my walls.

"Come on, Frankie," I mutter, unbuckling my seatbelt. "You can do this."

What's a little fighting?

Nothing, right? It's nothing.

Opening the door, I step out and look down at my outfit. It's a slight departure from my normal attire. Since this is a benefit, Helen and I will be accepting a check at the end on behalf of the shelter and I wanted to look nice. So, I dug through my measly closet and came up with a black shirt that falls off my shoulder and paired it with some skinny jeans and my only pair of pumps, which happen to be red.

It's not runway material, but it's a far cry from scrubs or jeans and a T-shirt.

When I get to the main entrance, the jitters in my stomach kick up a notch. One of the men working the doors looks a lot like Gunnar. As I hand him my ticket, he gives me a smile.

"Enjoy the fight."

I want to make conversation and ask him if he's Vali, but I can't. My anxiety has my mouth on lockdown, so I awkwardly brush my hair behind my ear and give him what I hope isn't a grimace.

There are people everywhere; more people than I thought would be here. I mean, I knew the numbers Gunnar ran by me when he was explaining how much money the shelter would be receiving, but seeing those numbers represented in people is . . . impressive.

As I make my way through the corridor, looking for the number that corresponds to what's on my ticket, I try to redirect my mind. *Think about the money, think about the shelter, think about all the women and children who will be helped because of tonight.*

My stomach drops a little at that thought, because the one mother and child I'd really love to help are still nowhere to be found. The police reported they've had a spotting of a black Ford truck that meets the description I gave, but when it was pulled over, only a man was driving. He didn't fit the vague description I was able to give of the guy I saw force them into the truck. My only hope now is Lisa finds a way to escape and makes her way back to us.

I hate it.

I want to be able to do more.

But now, I just have to pray they're safe.

The similarities between her and my mother continue, but I hope for Allie's sake, they don't spend the next ten years on the run. Never having a place that's truly yours really messes with your psyche. I tried to pretend none of it mattered, but it was a lie—just like so many other things about my childhood.

"Are you ready?" An announcer's voice booms through the venue, answered by a crowd of cheers. Hoots and hollers echo around me and I pace my breathing as I try to find Helen in the mass of people.

When she sees me, she waves. Her dark hair, normally styled in a tight bun, is loose and framing her jaw. I smile for what might be the first time today. Helen is really pretty. I've always known that, but it just hits me when her pale blue eyes find mine. She looks younger tonight, more relaxed. Maybe she always looks this way when she's not at the shelter? I wouldn't know, because once again, I leave her in a box.

Helen is my safe place.

The shelter is my safe place.

So, they stay together.

"I thought maybe you were going to stand me up," she says with a wink. Yeah, this Helen is much more relaxed. "And you look *hot*." The word *hot* coming out of her mouth sounds foreign. I'm a twenty-five-year-old who could get away with saying it, and even I don't say it. But, then again, I'm kind of a fifty-year-old in a twenty-five-year-old's body.

I feel the blush spread from my cheeks to my neck. This is probably why I always wear scrubs or jeans and t-shirts. Unnecessary attention makes me feel uncomfortable.

"Thanks," I manage to squeeze out, setting my bag on the floor by my chair. The bright lights of the arena catch my attention and my gaze travels to the cage.

Whoa.

"I'm assuming you didn't dress this way for me, though," Helen says. Her eyes follow mine to the cage and then past it, to where Gunnar is standing with his brother on the other side. His muscled arms and chest stretch out a white t-shirt as Cage wraps his knuckles in tape. The two brothers seem to share a moment. Cage ruffles Gunnar's hair, like he's twelve, and they both laugh it off. When the guy from the door walks up to join them, I know my assumption was right: he's Vali.

"How many brothers are there?" Helen asks, her voice sounding a little distant. "And is there one my age?"

My chest fills with air and I laugh. It feels good, like I've been strapped in a corset and someone just cut the laces. Not that I've ever been in a corset, but I can only imagine. It's just what I needed: something to take the edge off and distract me from this fight—from myself.

I lose track of Gunnar as people begin to move around, obviously getting ready for the event to start. My heart does this funny flip thing when I think about him in the ring. The announcer begins to pump up the crowd, getting them primed for the bout getting ready to take place. Helen explains there will be five fights in total, with Gunnar going last.

Awesome.

A few minutes later, the lights dim as music starts to blast through the speakers, causing the venue to erupt in applause. Spotlights bathe a dark hallway in light. The cadence of the music increases and my heart keeps rhythm. *Ba-bum, ba-bum, ba-bum.*

When a guy comes out of the hallway, arms raised in the air, the crowd goes wild.

"From Knoxville, Tennessee, weighing in at two hundred and thirty-five, Trevooooooor 'The Train' Tremellllllll." It's exaggerated, and for a moment I smile at the excitement. Everyone is so into it, buying into the hype and cheering as Trevor "The Train" Tremell makes his way into the ring. A man in a striped shirt checks his gloves and looks in his mouth before patting him down, like he's checking for weapons.

Then, the lights drop and the music changes. A guy in a white robe appears in the hallway. His head is bent as he walks slowly into the arena, a signature song reflecting his vibe filling the air—somber and ethereal. When the beat drops, he flips his hood back and punches the air.

Theatrical much?

"Isn't this exciting," Helen says, clapping with wide eyes as she takes it all in. When I don't say anything, she turns to me and leans in. "You okay?"

Before answering with an automatic lie, I check myself. This is Helen and there's no need to pretend, but I reply, "I'm fine." And I mean it. It's not so bad, more like a show; like a movie. Everything is larger than life and it makes it easy for me to separate myself from all of it.

I've never been to a sporting event, not even a high school football game. It just wasn't my scene, but I can imagine they're all like this—lively and energized.

I can do this.

Trevor "The Train" Tremell knocks his opponent out in less than thirty seconds.

I've never seen anything like it. They dance around each other for a few moments and then, *BAM*. It's so fast I can barely see it, like lightning. My heart practically leaps out of my chest. The nurse in me wants to rush the cage and tend to the guy lying there as the referee pounds the mat beside him, counting down to his fate.

"Five, four, three . . ."

Closing my eyes, I bring my hands up in a praying motion. "Please don't get up, please don't get up."

"Two, one."

Everyone around me goes crazy but I just exhale, thankful one fight is down. Hopefully, Trevor's opponent is okay. I wouldn't doubt he has a concussion. When I open my eyes, I see him standing and my heart finally settles. He'll be okay. It was just a hard hit, precisely placed for the most damage.

Trained fighters.

Who wants to hurt someone for fun?

Gunnar. That's who.

My eyes flutter closed and I pray away the next four fights, his included. I just want to make it through this and go back to the bubble we've been in over the last week. It's been good between us. I finally feel comfortable enough to share things with him; not everything, but some things. And the few secrets I've shared, my nightmares included, he's taken in stride—not judging, not treating me differently.

He's just been there—supportive, caring, and listening.

"I'm going to get a drink," Helen announces. "Do you want anything?"

Shaking my head, I hold my stomach, which is still unsettled. "No, I'm good."

"When did you eat last?"

Shrugging, I give her a look that says, "Don't mother me." She likes to do that sometimes, but I don't want her to tonight. "Earlier, but I'm going to wait on Gunnar."

Her smile is slow, but she likes that answer and excuses her way down the row, not saying anything. I know she likes Gunnar and I know she thinks we make a cute couple. She's told me. But everything between Gunnar and me feels new and fresh and private. I find myself wanting to store up every moment we share in its own special box inside my head, saving them for days that aren't as good as the ones I've had over the last month.

Since he's walked into my life—literally, right into my ER—everything has been different.

He's pushed me out of my routine and out of my comfort zone.

I'm no longer living a solitary life with moments of companionship. Gunnar has become my companion, maybe more. Definitely more. My feelings for him, which were so guarded and reluctant in the beginning, have been there all along and are beginning to bloom like a late-spring bud. The protective outer layer is peeling back, and beneath it is something that feels beautiful and special.

Once in a lifetime.

"Brought you a Coke," Helen announces as she makes her way back to her seat. "I can't have you fainting from low-blood sugar on my watch."

Shaking my head, I accept the drink and indulge her by taking a sip. It's good. The fizzy cold liquid sugar slides down my throat and is probably just what the doctor ordered. I use it as a distraction through the next couple of fights—taking a sip, watching the bubbles, picking at the edge of the cup. It's easier to control my impulses if I don't watch.

Before the fourth bout starts, I've finished my Coke and have a good excuse to go to the bathroom, so I do. I take my time; there's a bit of a line and I insist on two elderly women going ahead of me. They've been there and done that and are still standing to testify. I respect that.

"It's so exciting," one grey-haired woman says, locking herself in a stall. "My heart was beating out of my chest, but I haven't had this much adrenaline coursing through my veins since we went skydiving in eighty-five."

Skydiving?

"And did you see the muscles on the one in the blue shorts?" the other grey-haired woman asks. We'll call her Ethel, because she has a red hue to her grey. "Can you imagine the things he can do with those muscles?"

Her wistful tone has me biting back a smile.

Old women, man. You've gotta love their lack of filter.

A stall opens up and I take it, thankful for the privacy when the other finally replies, "I know what I'd like him to do with those muscles." Both ladies crack up laughing, water turning on and drowning out their cackles as I allow myself a quiet laugh in the bathroom stall.

I slip back into my seat, and Helen informs me the fourth bout ended while I was in the bathroom. Once again, it only went one round and ended in a knockout. I concentrate on taking slow, even breaths—in through my nose, and out through my mouth.

When the lights drop one last time, the music starts and my heart pounds in my chest.

Helen must sense my struggle because she reaches over and squeezes my arm gently. "It'll probably be over before you know it." Her smile is encouraging and meant to calm, but it doesn't. I'm not sure anything would calm me right now, except for the announcer coming out and letting us know there won't be a final fight. I can only imagine what the crowd would say to that. There'd probably be a riot of sorts, demanding what they came here to see.

"Gunnar 'The Show' Ericksonnnnnnn…"

Snapping my head up, I see him step into the ring, his eyes scanning the audience before landing on me. He doesn't smile; that's not part of his persona while he's up there. I can tell. He's different—focused, in the zone. The fun-loving, easy-going guy I've come to know and love isn't here.

Love?

Do I love Gunnar?

I definitely care about him and for him. His well-being means a lot to me. And at the end of the day, regardless if it's been good or bad, he's the person I want to see. If that's what it means to love someone, then yes, I love Gunnar.

Bringing my hand up, I rub at my chest, right where my heart beats wildly beneath the surface.

I love Gunnar.

How did that happen?

When did that happen?

"Are you okay?" Helen asks, drawing me out of my thoughts. Blinking, I turn to her as I swallow down this new realization. "Frankie?"

"I'm fine," I tell her. It's the same response as earlier, I know, but it's all I can manage.

I'm fine, I'm fine, I'm fine.

"It hasn't even started yet," she says matter-of-factly. "Loosen up a little." Helen's tough love approach has snapped me out of a lot of things over the years, but I don't know if it's going to work today. "This too shall pass," she continues. "It's an event, Frankie, a moment, not a life sentence. You're not going to die from this, and neither is anyone else. I don't know what goes on in that head of yours, but sometimes, you've just gotta tell those voices to shut the hell up."

I take a deep breath, nodding.

She's right. I know she's right. I'm an intelligent, well-educated woman. Ninety percent of the time, I'm also rational and level-headed. But then, something happens that shakes me to my core and I have zero control over it. I can't explain it away or stop it from happening, even when I so desperately want to.

When the buzzer sounds and the bout begins, I try to keep my focus on Gunnar, willing him to end this quickly and then feeling extremely guilty for wishing pain on a complete stranger. I didn't even hear the other guy's name. I was too busy locked up inside my brain.

At first, I'm able to steady my composure, almost going into a zone, my eyes trained on Gunnar's strong-set jaw and feeling in awe of the power oozing off him. His muscles tense and react as his feet begin to move, bouncing around the mat, as he and his opponent face off.

But then.

Everything suddenly feels like slow-motion—like quicksand.

Gunnar's opponent throws the first punch but it doesn't make contact. The crowd starts getting louder and everything speeds up, my senses on full alert. We're so close I can hear Gunnar grunt as he twists his body, his right fist coming around so fast the guy can't deflect. Sweat flies as his head snaps back, but then he's back for more.

A second later, it's Gunnar's head flying back as his opponent surprises him with a kick.

The look on Gunnar's face is lethal, bloodthirsty, and I wish I could unsee it because it stirs my deepest fears, the ones born in my nightmares. When he lunges out, releasing his fury on his opponent, all I can see is a whirlwind of fists and sweat mixed with blood. The cheers and jeers from the crowd are amplified and everything breaks into chaos—around me and inside me.

Flashes of reality mixed with fantasy flood my mind, and I have trouble deciphering where one ends and the other begins. My insides begin to tremor, like when you're so, so cold and you can't get warm, so your muscles tense in an effort to generate heat. But my stomach is burning with acid, and the stark contrast is too much.

I have to get out of here.

I can't do this.

"I have to go," I say to Helen, or whoever's listening, as I grab my bag and force my way out of the aisle and out of the venue. When I push through the glass doors, I gasp for breath like I've been running a marathon. My lungs are burning.

My throat feels like it's closing and I have to remind myself that I'm fine—I can breathe, I'm not dying. *I'mfineI'mfineI'mfine.*

Somehow, I make it to my car and start it up, resting my head on the steering wheel for a moment, trying to control my breathing . . . counting heartbeats . . . But when that doesn't do the trick, I back out and get as far from the venue as possible.

It's dark and I'm approaching the edges of Green Valley before my body finally starts to relax, but then I feel exhausted. My muscles feel spent and my brain and heart have practically given out.

When I pass the old corner store, I breathe even easier. I'm almost home. That's my goal at this point: get home. Then, I can allow myself to think about what happened and what it means... and about all the other questions and problems plaguing me.

How can I ever look at Gunnar the same?

How can I compartmentalize that?

The answer is simple: *I can't.*

I can't imagine living through that, time and time again. So, if I can't imagine that—can't even go there, have no desire to, and would rather cut off my right arm than sit through that again—then *what am I doing with him?*

My heart breaks at the thought. An elephant has taken up residence on my chest and it's physically challenging for me to draw breaths.

Breathe, Frankie.

Breathe.

I can't ask him to give up that part of his life for me. It's not just a hobby, it's his livelihood. It's what brought him to Green Valley. It's what he'll do after he leaves here . . . after he leaves me.

The roar of a motorcycle cuts my thoughts short and I feel the fresh rush of adrenaline burn through me before relaxing back into my seat.

They're no longer an issue.

They can't use me.

As I pull up to the stop sign, the bike idles behind me, practically right on my bumper, and I roll away from the intersection slowly. When I turn, so does he, and I wonder who it is and why he's following me.

I'd gotten the impression the order to no longer use my services had come from the top, whoever that is. After all these times of me helping the Iron Wraiths, I've only caught names in passing. I don't know who's in charge. There's never just one person who finds me. Sure, I've seen the same faces over and over, but our interactions are more like business transactions, with me always getting the short end of the stick.

Instead of turning down my street, I keep going to the next.

He follows.

When I turn back out on the main road, he follows.

Deciding to just get this over with and put an end to this miserable, weird, exhausting day, I pull into the parking lot of the Piggly Wiggly and throw my car in park. I'm not getting out, because I'm not that stupid. He can come to me. But I sit and wait with my window rolled down. The sound of boots crunching small pieces of gravel has me closing my eyes.

A man in a leather vest walks toward me, but I'm small . . . so, so small. He's huge, towering over me, and I'm crying. My throat hurts from trying not to cry because he told me not to, but I can't stop it. He reaches for me, but then someone stands in his way, blocking him from getting to me.

Blinking to try and clear the memory, I swallow as two hands appear on my open window, half-finger black gloves covering dirty hands.

Blonde hair flies as my mother is violently hit and thrown to the ground beside me. I scramble over to her, crawling on my knees but feeling the burn from fresh cuts on my legs. "Mommy . . .Mommy . . . please get up . . .get up," I beg, trying to shield her from the man standing over us. But I'm too small and he's too big. He pushes me out of the way and grabs her by her shoulders, sitting her up, only to slap her and making her bleed. My vision goes blurry and everything goes dark.

"Frankie?"

Shaking. My entire body is shaking again as I struggle to turn the memory off, trying to focus on the issue at hand.

"You're not supposed to talk to me anymore." My words come out wobbly and I don't sound like myself. It's far away. Everything seems so far away. "He said you're not supposed to talk to me . . . don't follow me anymore."

The boots shuffle against the gravel again and I cringe against the unwanted visual that now accompanies the sound. "I'm not gonna hurt you . . . and I'm tired of people telling me what to do."

I glance up to see a somewhat familiar face. The headlight from his bike illuminates him and the badge on his leather vest. *Crow.*

Can't say I've ever heard anyone say his name before. When I'm at the compound, I keep my head down, do the job, and get out. So, it's no surprise that I didn't know it until now.

"What do you want with me?" I ask, tears threatening to break. I'm not typically a crier. Over the course of my life, I can only think of a few instances where I've actually shed tears—when I failed my first test in college, the night before my nursing exam, and when my first patient died. All were moments where I felt completely over-whelmed.

Which is exactly how I'm feeling right now.

"What do you want with me?" I ask again, my voice sounding a bit unhinged. When I look up and make eye contact, Crow is watching me warily as he takes a step back. "You're tired of everyone telling you what to do. What does that mean?"

"I just want you to know who your father is."

CHAPTER 21

GUNNAR

I knew something was wrong when I searched the crowd for her after the fight and found her seat empty. Something in my gut—some connection to her—told me she'd left. Then I saw the look on Helen's face and I knew it wasn't good.

Helen's usual no-nonsense, all-business demeanor is missing tonight. In its place is a more real, expressive Helen. When we lock eyes, she shakes her head in silent communication—*she's not here. She's gone.*

Looking past Helen and toward the back of the venue, I scan the crowd for any sign of Frankie. If she's still in the building, I wouldn't hesitate jumping this cage and going after her, but there's nothing.

"Congrats, bro," Cage says, wrapping a towel around my neck and holding up a bottle of water. "Great fight. That combo at the end was killer—" He continues to give a recap of my entire bout, but after a few moments, realizes he lost me. "You alright?"

"Fine," I tell him, still searching. "Frankie left."

He glances back over his shoulder, toward where Helen is sitting, and sees the seat next to her is empty. "Maybe she got called in for work?"

"Maybe," I say, hoping it's something as easy as that.

Vali shows up at the gate, grinning up at us. "Hell of a fight, man. Best I've seen in a long time." His eyes turn to Cage and then back to me, a grin on his face. "You might even be better than this fucker."

"I can still kick your ass," Cage retorts, brushing it off as he turns back to me. "Let's get this wrapped up. We've still got to break everything down." It's been a long couple of days and all I really want to do is bail and find Frankie. My phone is in my dressing room and I'm desperate to see if she left me a text.

My mind goes to the first text message I sent to her just a few days ago.

I miss you.

She messaged me back a while later. *How can you miss me? You just saw me.*

The answer was easy for me, but harder to explain to her. I'd missed her the second she walked out of Daisy's and got in her car. I missed her sometimes when I even thought about being apart from her. I've been thinking about the future, what comes next. I came here to train with Cage, to be better, and win fights. I didn't come here to fall in love, but that's exactly what I'd done. And I don't regret it, but it's left me feeling a bit torn lately.

"Let's present this check," Cage says, checking my shoulder and pulling me out of my thoughts. "You good?"

I nod, taking the towel from my shoulders and wiping my face. This isn't how I'd pictured this moment. The fear that Frankie and fighting wouldn't mix has been something I haven't been able to shake, like an annoying mosquito buzzing around my face. One second I would swat it away—convincing myself we're more than that—and then it'd be back with a vengeance—telling me I don't know shit.

Maybe it—the fear—was right.

When Helen walks up and into the ring, she's wearing a tight smile. The lights are bright and everyone's eyes are on us, so I try to plaster on what I hope is a happy expression. I just won a fight.

We've raised a lot of money for a good cause. I should be happy. Frankie should be happy. She should also be here.

But she's not.

Cage begins to speak into the microphone, gaining the still-lingering crowd's attention, but not mine. Leaning over, I whisper to Helen, "Where is she?"

"She said she had to go," she whispers back, keeping her eyes forward.

"Was she okay?" The need to run to the back and grab my phone is consuming me. Twisting my neck one way and then the other, I try to release the tension. I'm always amped up after a fight, but this is worse. My skin feels like it could literally crawl right off my body and walk away. After Frankie.

"We'd like to present this check in the amount of forty-seven-thousand-dollars to the Women's Shelter of Maryville. Here to accept it is the director, Helen Murphy."

Helen steps forward and claims the check, turning back to look at me. Normally, I might say a few words, thank people for coming out to the fight and for their support. But not tonight. I'm not feeling my usual high. Tonight, I just want to be done so I can go find Frankie, or at least call her and hear her voice to settle this unease in the pit of my stomach.

Suddenly, the crowd erupts. Helen must have said something about the fight in her speech, and I missed it. But I can't miss the way everyone is now chanting my name. Honestly, I didn't think anyone would know who I am. Even though I was on the ticket as the main event, I'm no one around here. If this was in Dallas, or just about anywhere in the state of Texas, I'd expect the support. I've been fighting since I was a kid, trailing Cage to every event. I'm close to becoming a household name, like Cage. But not in the middle of Tennessee. Guess the Erickson name travels further than I thought. I have my brothers to thank for that.

Helen looks over her shoulder at me and then Cage, looking for direction.

Cage tilts his head at me, silently telling me this is it—this is what I've been waiting for, and I should take my moment. Tentatively, I step forward and the roar skyrockets. Pulling a canned speech out of my ass, one similar to what I've heard Cage make a hundred times, I say, "Thank you so much for coming out tonight. Your support means the world to me. MMA fans are the best fans in the world. None of us would want to come out and fight for an empty venue, especially not on a night like tonight. Not only did we get to enjoy a sport we love, but we helped a great cause along the way."

Dipping my head and giving a wave, I humbly accept their praise, turning the microphone back over to my brother Vali, who says a few more parting words before the music kicks back up and everyone starts to file out.

"Was she okay?" I ask Helen again when the mics are off and it's just the four of us—her, me, Cage, and Vali. "Did she seem upset?"

"I don't know," Helen says with a sigh. "She seemed to be handling it all well, but you know Frankie, she's good at hiding. Maybe it wasn't a good idea for her to come."

The way her brows are drawn and her expression is dim, I know she's worried too, which makes me worried even more.

"I'll call her," I assure Helen. "And if she doesn't answer before I get back to Green Valley, I'll go by and check on her."

"If you don't find her, I can check with the hospital and see if she was called in to work," Helen adds.

I nod, trying not to let the worry take over. *She's fine.* "Thanks."

"Thank you," Helen says, locking me down with her eyes and holding it for a moment before clearing her throat and plastering on a smile. "Thank you to all three of you. I'm so grateful for your help. This," she says, holding up the check, "is going to help so many people. You should all feel so proud of what you've accomplished." Glancing back to me and then to Cage and Vali, she continues, "I have to say, that was the most fun and excitement I've had in a long time."

We might not have made a fan out of Frankie, but Helen is definitely a convert.

The three of us laugh as we all walk out of the cage, heading our separate ways—me to the dressing room to find my phone, Vali to direct the teardown, and Cage to check in with security, making sure the place is cleared out, and walking Helen to her car.

Once I'm down the hall, I break out into a run, not stopping until I get to the dressing room. I dig through my bag and I breathe a sigh of relief when my phone is in my hand, but my stomach drops when I look at the screen and there's nothing—no missed call, no text.

No *good job.*

No *sorry I had to leave.*

No message about being called into work.

Nothing.

Pressing my thumb on her name, I wait for the ring . . .and then it rings, and rings, and rings. A message eventually comes on, telling me she can't answer and please leave a message.

"Frankie," I start, pacing the room as I talk. "Uh, hey . . . I'm calling to see where you are. Helen said you had to leave and we're both worried about you." Rolling my eyes at my nerves, I huff out a breath and pinch the bridge of my nose. "Call me, okay? I don't really care why you left, I just want to talk to you, make sure you're alright." I hesitate for a moment, not wanting to hang up without putting all my thoughts and feelings out there, but I decide that's good enough for now.

After I end the call, I stuff my phone and everything else scattered around the room in my bag. Before I walk out, I turn around, giving the room one last glance. Disappointment has me shaking my head, mostly at myself. Earlier, when I was preparing for the fight, I kept wanting to call Frankie and ask her to come early and meet me here. Visions of her propped up on the counter, of me standing between her legs, devouring her, had filled my head. That's what I'd had planned, but I decided to wait until after the fight.

Calling out to Vali and Cage, I tell them I'm going to Green Valley to look for Frankie.

The worry and dread are coming back in full force as I slip into the cab of the truck and start it up.

What if something happened to her?

177

What if she's sick?

What if those fucking Iron Wraiths found her?

Got to her, or whatever the fuck they do?

Hitting my palm on the steering wheel, I mentally berate myself for not digging deeper where they're concerned. I was hoping to have a chance as time went on, but this past week has been so good. I didn't want to mess it up with talk of motorcycle clubs and what connection she has to them.

Please, God. Let her be okay.

Driving a little faster than I normally would, I make it back in record time. When I turn off the main road and then down Frankie's road, my heart starts beating double time.

What if she's here?

What if she's not here?

What if she's here and doesn't answer the door?

Seeing her Mustang in the drive calms the pounding in my chest a little, but I still need to see her. I need to know why she left and that she's okay, so I park the truck and hop out.

When I get to the front door, I exhale, trying to release the nerves as I wipe my palms down the front of my shorts before tapping lightly on the door. Holding my breath, I wait. She doesn't answer, so I knock again. This time, I lean in and place my ear on the door.

Eventually, I hear movement on the other side and step back, not wanting to crowd her or scare her. It takes a few more seconds, but the door finally opens, and there she is in a baggy t-shirt and sweats, looking more beautiful than ever before.

But it's her eyes that get me.

They won't make contact with mine and she's holding the door as a barrier between us.

"Frankie?" I ask, my voice dropping low as I lean down to try and get her to look at me. "What's wrong? Are you okay? Did something happen?"

She visibly swallows and then licks her bottom lip, bringing her head up, but averting her eyes past me. "I'm sorry . . . I, uh . . ."

Pausing, she inhales deeply and closes her eyes before continuing. "I had to leave."

It's then I notice she's been crying and I turn to look behind me, trying to figure out where her distress is coming from. Surely, it's not me. I would never hurt her, but she looks like she's ready to bolt the door to keep out the bad people.

"Why did you have to leave? Talk to me." I try to keep my tone gentle, non-threatening. She should know by now she can tell me anything. I'd never judge her or demean her. Nothing she could say would drive me away. "Hey . . ." When I go to reach out and touch her—*needing to touch her*—she backs up an inch and that's when I see it: fear.

Of me.

Fuck.

"Are . . ." I swallow, forcing the bile back down into my stomach. This fucking kills me, but I have to get it out. "Are you afraid of me? Is that what this is about? The fight? Did something happen?"

She shakes her head and a tear slips down her cheek. She wipes it away, not looking at me, and says, "I just need some time. There's . . . I have a lot . . ." Pinching her lips together, she shakes her head again. "I just need some time."

Then she's gone. The door is shut and I hear the deadbolt slide back into place.

She's shut me out.

And this time, I'm afraid it's for good.

CHAPTER 22

FRANKIE

I've waited for as long as I can.

I've lived with lies and half-truths for far too long and I won't accept anything less than the whole story from my mother. Today is the day I learn everything.

Everything.

That word twists the existing knot in my stomach tighter.

After my run in with Crow last night and some of my own research on my computer, I'm pretty sure I know most of it. My mother is the only one who can fill in the missing pieces and stitch together the last of my frayed memory. Knowing the truth about my past will only do so much, though. I know that. It's only information. It'll be up to me what I do with it. I get to decide how my past affects my present and, ultimately, my future.

That's all I've ever wanted.

These are the thoughts that spur me on toward my mother's house, and I fully believe in them, but they do nothing to calm the emotional storm brewing inside of me.

When Gunnar stopped by my house, I wanted to hide and pretend I wasn't there, but I know him and I knew he wouldn't stop. He'd have the cops showing up and breaking down my door. So, I answered, but I wish I hadn't. Facing the cops would've been better than facing him. My heart wanted to reach for him while my mind wanted to run. It was the worst feeling.

Clenching my stomach, I try to focus on the passing trees to keep from being sick.

I haven't eaten or slept since yesterday morning.

Last night, after asking Gunnar to leave, my body felt exhausted. The tears I'd been mostly able to hold off fell freely and I'd tried to close my eyes to avoid thinking about how he'd looked when I turned him away. But my attempts at sleep were useless. Behind my closed lids were flashes of fists and blood, accompanied by my mother's screams. The wretched combination ensured I got no peace and no sleep.

Sometime around two o'clock, I gave up trying and I cleaned my house. And not your everyday cleaning, mind you. No, I tackled the deep cleaning—baseboards, ceiling fans, light fixtures, blinds—trying in vain to either erase the visions plaguing my mind or succumbing to sheer exhaustion.

Neither happened.

When the sky began to lighten, signaling the beginning of a new day, I'd made myself a pot of coffee and drank the entire thing while sitting on my back porch. Once the last drop was consumed, I'd decided I'd waited long enough and got in my car, which is where I am now.

As I drive down the highway, my earlier bravado starts to wane, and when I approach the turnoff that leads to the cabin, it feels like such a huge step.

I'm literally and metaphorically at a crossroads.

Easing my car onto the shoulder, I sit there.

I could turn around and head back to town and go back to living my life full of questions.

Now, I can see I've only been fooling myself all these years. I'd told myself I was fine, normal even, and dealing with the things in my past the best way I knew how. And that may have been true then, but it's not anymore.

Not since Gunnar Erickson walked into my life and pushed me out of my comfort zone.

He's changed me in so many ways—making me think differently, respond differently, allow someone in . . . allowing me to trust. He opened me up to new thoughts and feelings, things I thought were for other people, not me. He made me feel safe and secure and cared for, even when I didn't think those things were possible, up until last night.

Last night scared me.

The flashes of violence.

The shift in Gunnar's demeanor.

The fists.

The blood.

All of it.

I thought I could handle it, but I can't.

The logical side of my brain knows that's not Gunnar, not the real him. I should be able to compartmentalize—separating him from the fight—but I can't.

I want to, though.

And I think the first step in doing that is talking to my mother and getting the answers I deserve.

I need to handle my past so I can have a future.

This new me wants more. I'm tired of the fear and the running. I'm ready to face this head-on, regardless of the outcome or repercussions.

Turning my car down the tree-lined path, I take a deep breath, fortifying my resolve.

Deep down, I know Gunnar is good. *He's the best.* And I want to be with him. I want it so fucking badly. I just hope when all of this is over, he'll still be around.

Regardless, I have to do this for myself.

After parking my car in front of my mother's house, I take a deep breath and let it out, trying to mentally prepare for what awaits me inside her walls. I'm not sure what's worse: the fear of the unknown, or being afraid of what knowing the truth will do to me.

I walk up the steps, exhausted but resolved, determined to see this mission through. When the door opens, she takes one look at my disheveled self and steps back to let me in. "I'll fix us some tea," is all she says, before turning toward the kitchen, every bit as resolved as I am.

"I know who my father is." I know it's an awkward way to start this conversation, but I need to get it out, like poison from a snake bite. Besides that, she knows why I'm here. After our last visit, I knew I was close to uncovering the truth. So did she.

She doesn't respond for a long time. We're both sitting on her couch, blankets on our laps and teacups in our hands, not in a rush to have a conversation that's been a long-time coming.

"Who told you?" she finally asks.

"Some guy named Crow."

She nods her head slowly, swirling a spoon in her tea and not looking at me.

"I still don't know anything about him, about my childhood, and that's why I'm here. The nightmares are only getting worse and what I assume are memories are getting triggered more and more lately and I can't make sense of them. You have to fill in the blanks, Mom. I'm not a child anymore. You don't have to protect me." I want to add that she's *not* protecting me, she's only hurting me and making things worse, but I don't. Her pain has always felt worse than my own. "I deserve to know the truth."

She sighs, eyes trained on the tea, and then the words begin to tumble out like an avalanche. "I was always an outsider. I never fit in with anyone, but I wanted to. And because of that, I got mixed up with the wrong crowd. I did things I'm not proud of just to have a place to belong." She pauses, wincing. "Even though I knew the Iron Wraiths were bad news, I thought they'd be my friends—my family—as long as I stayed loyal and did what they asked. When Razor Dennings showed interest in me, I thought I'd won the lottery. The *leader* of the Wraiths wanted *me* and I thought that made me special. When I found out I was pregnant with you . . . well, it was the best day of my life. I was gonna have a baby, someone to love and take care of, and we were gonna be protected by the most powerful and feared man in town. I truly believed that . . . until his old lady, Christine, made herself known."

"You didn't know he had an old lady?" I ask, dread filling my stomach for her. I don't know much about the club, but I know you don't mess with someone else's man.

She shakes her head. "I was so young, so stupid and naive." She lets out a humorless laugh. "I figured Razor wasn't exactly faithful to me, but he spent so much time with me in the beginning, I'd assumed I was his favorite. I didn't know about Christine until she found me and threatened to slit my throat. I ran to Razor and told him what she'd said and he laughed. He laughed in my face, like I meant nothing to him, which was exactly what I'd meant—nothing. Less than nothing." When she pauses this time, I can feel her pain. I feel her want and need to belong to someone and then how it must've felt to have those needs crushed.

"I almost told him then I was pregnant but something inside told me not to. I must've known on some level it wouldn't have made a difference to him and might've given Christine even more ammo against me, so I left."

We're both quiet for a few minutes, letting the beginning of her story settle around us, while we prepare for the remainder. Because even though my mom knows what happens next, she's just as reluctant to continue as I am to hear it.

"Those first few years with you were so hard. Not because of you —you were the best baby a mama could've wished for. But being a poor single mother in a small town like ours wasn't easy. I didn't have any help and struggled to keep a job for more than a few months at a time, which means I didn't have money for a place to live or food or medicine. I'd latch onto men who meant nothing to me just for a place for us to stay but they all got tired of us, and eventually, we'd be on the streets again."

As I listen to her talk about our lives back then, I'm still amazed I don't remember any of this. It's as if she's talking about someone else or reading a story to me. None of it is familiar, but I'm starting to understand more and more.

"You were almost seven when I couldn't take it any longer. We were always hungry, always dirty, and your school was threatening to call social services on me. I couldn't lose you and I knew they'd take you away if they knew we didn't have a permanent place to live, so I did the only thing I could think of—I went back to the Iron Wraiths."

At her words, I feel my spine stiffen and my skin go cold. This is the part of the story that changes everything—I just know it. This is the *everything* I both want and dread.

"I thought enough time had passed that I'd be welcomed back, that all would be forgiven. I thought Razor would be thrilled to know he had another kid to raise—"

"Stop right there," I command. "Razor has other children? I have brothers and sisters?" I'm not sure how to feel about this information. It's overwhelming, to say the least, but that's been the last twenty-four hours. The nurse in me thinks I might be in shock, but I just need to press on a little longer.

We're almost there.

"Yes, I guess you do. I don't think about it much now but back then, I was happy you might have siblings to play with. But, anyway," she continues her story, "Razor was a man's man, your typical alpha male, you could say, and most men like that feel the more offspring they have, the more virile and powerful they are. I thought he'd . . . well, I thought he'd love you. I didn't care if he loved me or not, but how could he not love our perfect little girl?"

My mother wipes her eyes and I notice her hands are shaking. I'm torn between wanting to comfort her and wanting to shake her so she'll keep talking. I swear, this is the most I've ever heard her say in all my life.

"I was desperate. So desperate . . ." She trails off briefly before shaking herself out of her thoughts. "Turns out, Razor isn't an alpha male—he's a monster."

Her voice is quivering and I'm afraid she's going to fall apart.

"It's alright, Mama." Reaching over, I place my hand over hers.

"You're doing great, just please keep going. I'm okay and you're okay. We're safe."

She nods, wiping her eyes before continuing, "I found a dress for you at the shelter and brushed your hair into a ponytail, so he'd see how pretty you are." Finally, she looks up at me, giving me a watery smile. "But when I presented you to him, he laughed. It wasn't a laugh that made a person want to laugh along. It was the kind of laugh that made your stomach turn sour. It was the sound of evil, I know that now.

"He called me names—horrible names, some I'd never even heard before. He said I was stupid for coming back and bringing you to him. He said he didn't love any of his kids and he'd show me what they were good for. I . . . I had no idea . . ."

She's full-on crying now, so I pull her into my arms and try to soothe her, but she pushes away and shakes her head, as if to say, "No, I have to keep going."

Once an avalanche starts, it doesn't stop until it gets to the bottom of the mountain.

"He told me to get him a beer from the bar and leave you with him so he could get to know you better. I thought it was a good sign, but when I came back..." My mother's body shakes along with her sobs and I realize I'm crying, too. I'm not sure why but I've always cried when she cried. There's not much worse than seeing your mother cry.

"He'd cut you."

My blood turns to ice at her whispered words.

"When I came back with his beer, he had you laying on top of a table and he—he was . . . cutting you. Not stabbing, not slicing, but cutting your flesh. He was so meticulous about it, like it was some sort of art form. It took me a moment to realize what was really happening because there was no sound. Tears were running down your cheeks and your mouth was open in a silent scream. Seeing you like that still haunts my dreams."

The two of us remain quiet for a few minutes. My tea has gone cold, but I wouldn't be able to drink it now if I'd wanted to. I think it'll be quite a while before I'm able to eat or drink anything without the threat of vomiting.

Eventually, a question pops into my head.

"Razor gave me all these scars during that one time?" To my nurse's mind, that just doesn't seem possible. That's a lot of trauma for anyone to suffer through, much less a child.

I watch her sit back while keeping her eyes on her fingers as she twists them together. She waits a bit longer before answering me.

"That was the first time it happened, but it wasn't the last. His biker name is Razor for a reason. He cuts his children because it gives him some sick relief or pleasure, like he's claiming them . . . you. I thought that was what I wanted—for him to claim you—but I had no idea what I was really asking for." She pauses, shaking her head as her eyes drift away, obviously stuck in a horrid memory.

The ice in my blood starts to simmer now because I can't allow myself to believe what I think she's trying to say. Surely, I'm wrong.

"Frankie, I was in a bad place back then and I was a completely different person. I know there's no excuse but please, let me try to explain." When I don't respond, she continues. "I've already said how desperate and scared I was, but what I didn't say is that I was an addict, too. When I saw Razor working on you, it was easy to make myself believe it wasn't real, that I was just high or hallucinating. And when he was done, he gave me a wad of cash for us to live off for a few months. I had no idea the pattern I was inadvertently agreeing to."

"You let him cut on me for money? Is that what you're saying?" No longer simmering, my blood is now boiling.

"It wasn't like that!" she cries. "At least, I didn't mean for it to be. It wasn't until I was finally clean that I realized what I'd done, what *he'd* done. I walked in on him just like I had the first time except this time, my eyes were clear. And they saw red. I attacked him, jumped on his back, and pulled him off you. That's when he turned on me but I didn't care. By that time, I knew I'd deserved it and I was willing to face it again and again if it meant I was keeping you safe."

"That's my earliest memory now, him hitting you. Before the nightmares started, it was being welcomed into the shelter by Helen. Last night, I watched someone I care about fighting in a cage match and it brought back images of you being hit. I . . . I couldn't deal. I ran and then Crow found me, telling me about Razor. Everything has been such a mess inside my head. I don't know what to do with all of the newness, all the rawness of these memories. It's crazy that I blocked it all out. I don't remember anything from that time, not even getting my scars."

She places her hand on mine and I feel it shake, her old fears coming back in full force.

"Promise me you'll stay far away from them." There's a pleading in her tone and when our eyes meet, I see what drove her into hiding —the pain, the trauma. I might've spent my entire life hiding away the truth, but my mother lived it. She saw the horror and she remembers. It's what's kept her here for so long.

She tries to hide the new pain I've just caused by peeling the scabs off old wounds, but I can still see it, still hear it in her voice. "They're trouble, Frankie. All of them. I'll never be able to apologize enough for bringing you into a world like this. I tried for so long to keep you from it. Selfishly, I'd hoped you'd never remember and never find out about Razor because I couldn't bear you knowing the truth about *me*. I know that makes me a horrible mother, a horrible person, and I don't blame you for being angry with me."

When she pauses, I let her explanation soak in. At least, I try to. All this time, she's been trying to protect me, but what about then? What about when I was small and helpless? How could a mother allow a man to cut her own child? Those questions plague my mind as I stare at the mother I thought I knew and try so hard to reconcile her with the truths I've been faced with.

"I did what I thought was best . . . for you," she says absentmindedly, like she's lost to her thoughts and memories. As a sob breaks through, I instinctively reach for her, wanting to heal what's broken. "It probably sounds crazy to you, all of this, but it's true. I just hope you'll be able to forgive me one day."

189

CHAPTER 23

GUNNAR

*L*ying flat on my back on the mat, I drape an arm over my eyes and breathe deeply, recovering from the intense sparring session with Cage. Usually, I'm with Vince, but Cage was feeling left out and needed to release the demons. So, I indulged him.

Honestly, it was great. Even with his injured shoulder, which is what took him out of the sport professionally, he's still a beast to contend with.

His left hooks and roundhouse kicks are better than anyone else's I've ever come up against.

I appreciate this level of exhaustion; maybe I'll actually sleep tonight.

Ever since the fight, which was over a week ago, I spend every moment—when I'm not kicking ass or getting my ass kicked—thinking about Frankie and how I can fix this. She hasn't called or sent a text message and I've been waiting, trying to give her the space she asked for.

But I'm starting to think I could be waiting forever.

"Get this," Vali says walking into the studio, a newspaper in one hand and a half-eaten muffin in another. He's really made himself at home over the past couple of weeks and I'm starting to wonder if he ever plans on going back to Dallas. Not that I mind having him around; he's definitely brought some much-needed levity to my daily routine, refusing to let me dwell in the dark places.

He and Cage are constantly on my ass to stay focused and let the cards fall where they may—meaning Frankie—but that's easier said than done and they fucking know that. I know I can't force her to open up to me or let me in . . . but fuck it all if I don't want to try.

And it's *killing me* to not be able to see her, touch her . . . to know if she's okay.

Thanks to Helen, I know she's still going to work and the shelter, still carrying on with her life. Except for the part where I'm concerned. Helen won't give me much, but she assures me Frankie is "hanging in there." She also made me promise to not give up on her. I didn't plan on it, but I also didn't think it'd be almost two weeks of silence.

After shoving the rest of the muffin in his mouth and swallowing it down, Vali continues. "'The Viking sightings continue around Green Valley. Now, there is not only one Scandinavian Stud, but three. After a benefit fight in Maryville benefiting the Women's Shelter of Maryville and sponsored by Green Valley's newest establishment, Viking MMA, people around town have been abuzz about the Erickson brothers.'"

Vali lets out a loud laugh, holding the paper in the air like a trophy. "We made the front page of the *Green Valley Ledger*! I'm sending this paper to Mom. She'll love it."

I roll my eyes, pulling myself up into a crunch position. Might as well do some work while I'm down here. There's another fight next week and after winning so decisively in my last one, the media is swarming and talking. Now I know what Cage was always talking about when he said it was easier when he was an unknown name.

When people know what you're capable of, they expect it out of you every time. You don't get the luxury of fighting when you feel like it.

Right now, I definitely don't feel like it.

The only thing I feel like doing is hunting Frankie down and demanding she talk to me and let me help fix whatever is wrong.

"Oh, shit," Vali says, turning a page in the paper and then looking up at us. "We made the gossip column too." His eyes grow wide with excitement. No one appreciates the power of media more than Vali. He lives for shit like this.

He pauses, scanning the paper. "Apparently, Trixie—or maybe it's Tess, I don't know because they sign off with two names—anyway, one of them is wondering how many Ericksons there are and whether or not they're planning an invasion."

"I was kind of wondering the same thing," Cage says, walking back into the studio. "I thought you were just here to help with the benefit."

Vali looks up, a look of hurt on his face. It's fake, but he's playing it up well. "Are you trying to get rid of me? I fly all the way down here, forgo Starbucks for weeks, and sacrifice common amenities like late night drive-throughs, delivery services, Uber . . ." He's ticking them off as he makes a list. "Oh, and frozen yogurt. Dude, if someone wanted to make a killing, they'd open up a fro-yo shop."

Cage just rolls his eyes and shakes his head. "That doesn't answer the question."

"You didn't ask one," Vali retorts.

"How long are you planning on staying?"

"Why are you trying to get rid of me?"

"It's getting a little crowded," Cage shoots back with a smirk.

"Well, someone's in a peachy mood. What? No midday sexcapades?"

Vali and I both share a look and he chuckles. We all love giving each other shit, but Cage is right. With the three of us and Tempest, the quarters are crowded.

"I was actually thinking about putting an ad in the paper to see about finding a place to rent. Kind of like a roommate available ad," I say, continuing my crunches until I tap out at a hundred.

This time, it's Cage and Vali who exchange looks.

"What?" I ask. "It's a small town. We've established that. I spend all my days and nights here at the studio training, except for my occasional escape to the Piggly Wiggly. I have a fight in a week and no social engagements planned for the near future. If I want to find a place to live, I'm going to have to get creative."

Cage huffs, sitting down beside me on the mat. "I'm not sure if that's such a good idea. You need to focus on your fights."

"I'll go back to Dallas if that'll make it easier," Vali offers.

Pulling myself up, I lean over, resting on my knees. "I want to find a place. I like it here, so if I plan on staying, I need a place of my own. But I also want to save what money I have until I make it to some bigger tickets. So, finding a room to rent seems like my best bet. Besides, there are plenty of old people in this town who have an extra room. Maybe I'll luck out and get a little old grandma who wants to make me pies and shit."

"That's just what you need," Cage says, sucker-punching me. "I'm working to get you in the best shape of your life, and you're dreaming about pies."

It's not exactly what I'm dreaming about, but it feels good to have my mind off of the real issues for a few minutes. And I'm glad Vali is staying for a while, however long that may be. I like having him around.

"We've got a fight in Nashville in two weeks," Cage says, glancing up at me and then to Vali. "I thought we'd drive up the night before and get a hotel room so you're well-rested."

I nod in agreement.

"I need you to get your head on straight between now and then— whatever that takes. Cut ties, make amends, do one or the other, but make it happen."

Gritting my teeth, I stare at a large piece of tape on the mat, covering a tear. It's a gaping wound, kind of like the one Frankie left in her wake. I know Cage is right, but I hate him telling me what to do. It's none of his business what happens between me and Frankie. If she wants to talk about things before I leave for Nashville, I'll be elated, but if she doesn't, that's okay too.

I've thought about checking out the farmer's market or going to the Piggly Wiggly on Tuesday nights, but I don't want her to feel pressured or trapped. Or scared. Maybe I'm a little scared of seeing her again too. That look she gave me is one I won't forget for a long time, if ever.

Whatever she's working through is huge, I know that now. I mean, I had an idea before the night of the benefit, but I wasn't sure how deep it ran. Now, I know it runs bone-deep. At night, sometimes when I'm trying to sleep, I think about the nightmare she told me about and how badly I wished it was only that—a nightmare—but now I'm thinking it was real. The cuts, the blood, the hits, the screams . . .all of it. And it kills me.

I hope Helen is telling me the truth and that Frankie is okay.

She has to be okay, because if she's not okay, then I'm not okay.

The two of us are intertwined and at some point, I have to believe she'll find her way back to me.

CHAPTER 24

FRANKIE

*G*unnar: *I saw some wildflowers today and thought of you.*

I glance down at the text for probably the twentieth time since receiving it earlier today and smile. It's the same reaction I've had every time I look at it but with one exception: with every look, my smile grows. In fact, it's so big right now I don't even try to hide it when my therapist, Samantha, not-so-discreetly clears her throat.

"Is that a message from Gunnar?" she asks.

Glancing at the text one more time, I nod.

"Are you going to respond this time?"

I shake my head no and place my phone on the floor by my feet so I won't be tempted to look again. At least not until I'm home.

"Have you communicated with him at all since our sessions started?"

"I haven't seen him or spoken to him since the night of the benefit, which was almost a month ago."

"And why is that?"

Fighting the urge to roll my eyes, I pick at my fingernail instead. I know it's her job and the reason I'm here, but I really hate it when she's so blatant with her questioning. She might as well have me lay on her couch and talk about my sex dreams. Maybe her questions seem typical to me because of my medical background or maybe it's because, despite Samantha being a great therapist, I've been doing my own research into my issues and already know what to expect from our sessions.

"Because," I say, sighing. "He doesn't really know what he's getting into with me. Hell, I barely know what he's getting into, and I don't want him to feel like I'm a waste of time. I don't want him to regret me." My voice is smaller now but I know she hears me. The look of disappointment on her face tells me as much.

"He seems very smitten with you and if he thought he was wasting his time, he wouldn't still be texting you a month after last seeing you. Gunnar is an adult and his own person, so you can't make decisions for him. If you truly don't want to have contact with him, you need to let him know. It's wrong to string him along."

My face heats up with a mixture of anger and embarrassment. I don't mean to string him along; I just don't know how to face him after telling him to leave me alone.

"What if I gave you some homework to do with Gunnar?"

This catches my attention and I'm instantly interested in Samantha's idea. "What kind of homework?"

"Trust-building exercises," she replies.

"You're not going to make us do trust falls with each other, are you?"

Samantha laughs. "You scoff, but trust falls work. I promise."

"What are our other options?" I ask, ignoring her comment.

"You need to be honest with Gunnar and tell him what's going on with you, why you ran off, and how your childhood memories are affecting your adult relationships. Before you do that, though, you need to know you can trust him. This is the easy part." She gives me a genuine smile and I'm encouraged by her excitement over me considering her ideas.

"Sit across from each other and stare into each other's eye for three minutes."

"I don't know about that. It sounds really weird and uncomfortable." Although, I do miss Gunnar's sea-glass eyes . . . he has amazing eyes. Maybe it wouldn't be as bad as I think.

"It may be awkward at first, and it's perfectly fine to laugh a little. But after a while, it'll become easier and more meaningful. You can also send him on a very specific errand. Ask him to go to the store and buy a particular brand of food. Tell him to text you if the store doesn't have exactly what you tell him to get."

"I don't want to make him jump through hoops for me or boss him around."

"That's not what the exercise is about. It's to show *you* he can be trusted to do what you ask or get what you need."

I already know Gunnar would get me anything I ask for at a store, no question. This actually relieves me, makes me feel like we're already ahead of the game, even though he has no idea I'm even in therapy.

Shit. I really need to talk to him. The truth is, I'm dying to see him. I miss him so much, but I can't bear the thought of him looking at me with pity or disappointment in his eyes.

"Let's switch gears a bit," Samantha says. "Have you spoken with your mother recently?"

Another topic I'd like to avoid. *Super.*

"I still go to her house once a week to pick up the things she wants me to sell at the farmer's market, but we don't really talk. I'm just not sure what to say to her."

"Tell her how you feel. It's okay to still be angry with her, you know?"

"The crazy thing is, I don't think I *am* angry with her. Not anymore, at least." I'm not sure when my feelings changed, because Lord knows I was pissed after she told me about my father. But those harsh feelings have dissipated. Even though I hate what she did, what she put me through, I'm trying really hard not to judge her for her decisions. I've never been in her situation and I know she must've felt completely hopeless and lost. I also believe she feels true regret and remorse and did the best she could to turn our lives around after that night.

"But she thinks you are?"

"I guess. Probably . . ." My words trail off as I realize I'm hurting the two people who care the most about me by closing myself off. This is what happens when you're an emotional recluse, and it's the main reason I'm in therapy. I don't want to push people away. I want to love freely and openly without second-guessing every little thing.

Mostly, I want what everyone wants: to love and be loved in return.

BC

As I drive into work, I think about Gunnar. Not for the usual reasons, but for another homework exercise Samantha wants me to do. Because I'm so good at putting people and situations in their own little boxes, keeping them nice and tidy in my mind, Samantha thought it would be good to do the same thing with Gunnar and his fighting.

It was very alarming to hear Samantha describe my aversion to violence as almost obsessive, but the more I think about it, the more I'm starting to agree. Because I associate violence with what Razor did to me and my mom, I can't fathom why someone like Gunnar would want to participate in a violent act for fun or for a career. But, if I remind myself he's not a violent or angry person, he's not aggressive or hurtful, and most importantly, he's not Razor Dennings, it's easier to accept his fighting as sport.

Speaking of my father, I've recently learned he's on death row here in Tennessee for multiple murders with no chance for parole. That was the day I realized I needed to seek professional help. The confusion, hurt, and anger I felt morphed into a deep self-loathing until Samantha made me realize I had nothing to do with Razor's crimes. Why I thought I did, I have no idea, but it's a perfect example of how irrational I've been lately.

The other thing I've had to come to terms with was the fact the Wraiths lied to me for over two years, stringing me along and making me believe my father was somewhere behind the scenes, when in fact he wasn't. It should probably piss me off more than it does, but I can't find it in myself to care anymore. Most of the men are despicable excuses for human beings and I never should've put any amount of trust in them. I was chasing a dream—a pipe dream—and that's over now. No longer am I trying to find myself. I've been here all along, and it's up to me to decide what makes me feel happy and whole.

After clocking into my shift and leaving my things in my locker, I walk to the nurse's station to see what patient needs to be seen next.

"Hey, Frankie. There's a lady here who's been waiting to see you." Gladys, the ER receptionist, hands me a file with paperwork inside, explaining why the patient is here.

"Really? It must not be a medical emergency if she was willing to wait for me to get here."

Gladys shrugs then points across the room. "I'm just relaying the message. She and her little girl are over there in the waiting room."

A woman and little girl are here to see me?

Could it be Lisa and Allie?

I try not to get my hopes up, but still walk with great purpose across the ER and into the waiting room. I've barely made it inside the area when I hear my name being yelled by a sweet, little angel voice. I turn toward the voice and nearly fall on my knees at the sight of Lisa and Allie.

Rushing over, I quickly hug them both before assessing whether or not they were hurt. "Are you okay? Let me take you to triage. You shouldn't have waited for me if you need to see a doctor."

Lisa places her hands on my shoulders to get my attention. "We're fine, Frankie, I promise. I do have a favor to ask, though."

"Anything, just tell me what you need."

"We'd like to go back to the shelter. Could you bring us when your shift is over? We would've gone straight there but the hospital was closer. I remembered you saying you worked here so we came to see you and ask for help."

"Of course, I will. My shift just started, but I can take you when I get a break in a couple of hours. Would that be okay?"

"That would be fine, thank you."

I pull some cash out of my scrub pocket and hand it to Lisa. "Why don't you go get some food in the cafeteria while you wait? I'll come find you when my break starts."

I know Lisa doesn't want to take the money but she also has her daughter, Allie, to think about. There's no way I will let either one of them go hungry on my watch. "Take it," I implore. Eventually, she takes the cash and slips it into her pocket before hugging me again.

"Thank you so much," she whispers. She quickly wipes a stray tear from her eye and grabs Allie's hand, leading her down the hall to the cafeteria. I watch them until they turn a corner, relief filling my body with every step they take.

They're here, and they're safe.

I'm hit again with the similarities between Lisa and Allie and me and my mom. Lisa and my mom made decisions that put both mother and child in danger but I truly believe they thought they were doing the right thing, the best thing for them and their situation. Unfortunately, they were wrong and consequences were paid, but that's in the past now. Like Samantha says, the past can be nice to visit from time to time but if we truly want to live, we need to stay in the present.

After my shift is over, I take Lisa and Allie back to the shelter, assuring myself they're back and they're safe at least a dozen times. Helen is ecstatic to see them. The look she gives me as she welcomes them back in with open arms says she's just as relieved as I am. To her credit, she doesn't fuss over them, just shows them to their room.

The two of us share a quiet conversation out in the hall. "So they just showed up at the hospital?" she asks. She checks back at the closed door one last time, like she has to assure herself they're here and they're safe, too.

"Yeah," I reply, smoothing down my hair, which I'm sure looks atrocious after the long day. "I would've brought them back sooner, but it was a crazy day in the ER. I'm sure they're both exhausted."

"Well, they're back and they're—"

"Safe," we say in unison, giving each other a tired, weary smile.

Helen squeezes my hand. "You should get home. I'm sure you're beat."

I nod and tell her I'll see her soon. When I plop down in my car, all I can think about is driving to my mother's house so we can talk —really talk. Seeing Lisa stirred up things that have been left unsaid. I need my mother to know I've forgiven her, and I want to move forward, leaving the pain in the past.

But before I do that, I have a text to send. Pulling my phone out of my bag, I turn it on. Not surprisingly, there's a new text waiting from him. Unable to fight back the smile, I swipe to read it and my heart clenches in my chest. His words bring back the vivid memory of a vulnerable Gunnar showing up in my ER, kind of like Lisa and Allie did tonight. He didn't know if I'd throw him out or accept him.

I don't think, I don't worry, I don't do anything. I just start typing.

CHAPTER 25

GUNNAR

"You've got ten minutes," Cage calls out from the hallway. "I want you to have time to warm up and get in the zone."

I grunt from my spot on the floor of my dressing room at the venue in Nashville. It's a lot nicer than some of the other places I've fought at over the years. Unlike at the benefit fight, I'm not the main event tonight, but I am next to last. Typically I'd be sitting here with my earbuds in, losing myself to the music while I prepare for the fight. But instead, I'm staring at my phone, my thumb scrolling through the text messages I've sent Frankie.

Thirty-two.

That's how many messages I've sent Frankie, one a day since I last saw her. She hasn't replied once. At first, I didn't expect her to, but I still wanted her to know I was thinking of her. But now, I'm starting to feel desperate and hopeless, which isn't like me. I'm definitely a glass-half-full kind of person, but I've never been through something like this.

Before we left yesterday, I had to fight the urge to drive to her house. It was Friday, and I know she volunteers on Fridays, so I didn't do it. Even if it had been a day she was home, I still wouldn't have.

If and when Frankie decides to let me back in, I want it to be on her terms. I need to know she really wants it—us, *me*.

The separation between us has done nothing to dull the ache and need I have for her.

I want her.

Even her broken pieces and scars.

I just wish there was some way for me to break through her walls, once and for all.

A while back, Cage told me some people need to know you're going to be there when they fall. I felt that in my soul and like it was something Frankie needed, so I tried to give her that as best as I knew how. But then, after the benefit, everything went to shit and now I don't know what she wants or where we stand.

Glancing at the time, I see it's almost eight, so I quickly type out what I'm feeling in the moment. Over the past couple of weeks, my text messages to Frankie have become more like a journal, a place for me to leave my thoughts. They're all for her anyway. I don't care if they make me seem weak or desperate. I have nothing to hide.

Me: I miss you, so bad it hurts.

Me: I'm so confused why it all went wrong.

Me: Help me understand.

Me: Give me a chance to be there for you when you fall.

After hitting send on that last text, I toss my phone to the side.

"Five minutes," Vali hollers.

As I go to grab my hoodie from the floor, my phone chimes with an incoming message.

I swear to God, if Cage is texting me from the hallway again, he's a dead man.

If anyone ever thinks I'm too persistent, they've never met my brother. Growling, I grab my phone to silence his ass, but then I see the name and my breath catches in my throat.

Frankie.

My heart beats like crazy in my chest as I swipe my thumb across the screen to read the message.

Frankie: I miss you too.

It's just four words, but they're the best fucking four words I've ever read. They feel like a lifeline pulling me out of the deep.

My thumb hovers over the screen as I try to decide what to say. *What the fuck do I say?*

Do I not say anything at all?

Will it seem too eager or desperate if I tell her I feel like I just took my first real breath in over a month?

I'm still debating when Vali yells again for me to get my ass out there.

Unplugging my phone from the charger, where I typically leave it during a fight, I take it with me and run out the door. When I get to the hallway, Vali and Cage are both standing there giving me *the look*. The same one they've been giving me my entire life, like I'm inconveniencing them while simultaneously raining on their parade.

"Fuck off," I grunt, pushing past them. "I got a text message from Frankie."

They can give me all the shit they want. I don't care. Besides, I might be the little brother, but my day has come and I can officially kick both their asses.

Neither of them say a word as we walk down the hallway and into the holding area. All the while, I'm running possible responses through my head, none of them making the cut. As I'm staring at the words again, three little dots show up.

She's typing.

Unfortunately, they disappear as fast as they appeared and my heart sinks back down into my chest. Then they're back.

Frankie: Can we talk?

Letting out a laugh that's somewhere between relieved and pained, I run a hand through my hair and lean back against the wall. Of course she'd want to talk now, while I'm three hours away and getting ready to fight.

"What's up?" Cage asks, coming to stand in front of me, his

hands going to my shoulders as he starts to work me over to loosen me up. His eyes find mine and I see the concern. "Everything okay?"

Even though he's told me to cut ties with Frankie, deep down, he didn't really mean it. They might not know her very well, but Vali and Cage care about her well-being. If she means something to me, she means something to them. That's just how our family is.

"She wants to talk," I mutter, running a hand down my face and then back up, smoothing the hair that's tied back in a ponytail at the nape of my neck. To some people, this might seem like the worst kind of distraction, something I definitely don't need going into a fight, but it's the opposite for me.

Her reaching out is the best stress reliever I could've asked for. I feel like I can breathe again, like there's hope for us. It's a light at the end of this dark tunnel I've been in for the past month.

The only thing that would be better than these few words would be her right here by my side, but I can wait for that. I've waited this long—what's another day?

Quickly, I type out a response, letting her know I'm in Nashville. I don't bring up the fight because I don't know what kind of trigger it really is for her and until I know the details of what she's dealing with, I don't want to make matters worse.

Me: I'll text you as soon as I'm back in Green Valley.

When I came to Tennessee a few months ago, I didn't have any solid plans for how long I'd be here. All I knew was I wanted to train with Cage. Frankie was unexpected, but aren't all the best things in life?

The easy part is that I can choose anywhere in the world for a home base, and I choose her. Wherever Frankie is, as long as she'll have me, that's where I want to be.

Is it too much? Too soon? Especially since I don't even know her entire story? Maybe, but I can't help my feelings and I can't help what my heart wants.

I've always been an all-or-nothing kind of person, and I know I want all of Frankie.

CHAPTER 26

FRANKIE

*I*t's early, sometime between night and morning, and I'm pacing my living room—walking from one end to the other, stopping briefly to look out the window.

Gunnar sent me a text fifteen minutes ago, letting me know he'd made it back to Green Valley and asked me to text him when I woke up. I was already awake and thinking of him, so I sent a text back right away telling him I wanted to talk whenever he could. I explained that my shift starts at eight, so anytime between now and then would works for me, unless he wanted to wait, to which he replied: *Now??*

That sequence of events led to this—pacing.

Glancing at the clock on the stove in the kitchen, which is visible from here, I see it's almost three-thirty. I know he'll be here. He said he would and he's never given me a reason to doubt him, so why am I so nervous?

Because it's been a month.

Because I have so much to tell him.

Because I love him.

Because I'm afraid he'll decide this is all too much and tell me to have a nice life, but he's going to have to pass.

"Calm down, Frankie," I mutter to myself, bringing my thumb up to my mouth to chew on my fingernail. "It's going to be fine. He's going to be here and you're going to tell him everything you've been wanting to tell him and then you'll deal with whatever happens next."

One of the things Samantha and I have been working on is overcoming avoidance. Apparently, I've used it for so long I don't even realize when I'm doing it. In addition to deep breathing and focusing on relaxing when faced with something that's uncomfortable, she wants me to basically talk myself down. *I'm fine. I can do this.* My favorite one is: *no bad thing can last forever.*

Not even Razor Dennings.

He's on death row.

That information actually helps me sleep better at night. When I wake from the nightmares—which I still have occasionally—I remind myself that he's no longer able to hurt me, my mother, or anyone else.

After I texted Gunnar back last night for the first time in over a month, I felt a huge sense of relief.

I could say I wish I'd done it sooner, but I wasn't ready. A few weeks ago, I promised myself I wouldn't reach out to him until I was, because he's good and kind and generous and he deserves the best. He deserves *my* best.

I'm still not quite there, but I'd like to continue to work on it. With him. If he'll have me.

Headlights flash through my front windows and I rush to the door. Nervous excitement courses through me along with another wave of relief. So much relief. He said he'd be here, and he is.

If Samantha has helped me in any way, she's made me more aware of myself, helping me realize what I need to feel safe—trust being the most important thing. Without trust, there's no safety, and without safety, there's no potential for a relationship.

By Gunnar showing up here, he's passed a test he didn't even know he was taking.

There's a light tap on the door and I press my hand to it, bracing myself with a deep breath and another round of positive affirmation. *I can do this. He deserves the truth. All my truths.*

After unlocking the door, I slowly open it, my heart beating faster with fears of the unknown. But I do it, and good God, am I happy I took the leap. He's standing on my front porch with a pensive expression, hands tucked in the front pockets of his jeans, with a white t-shirt on top and freshly washed hair . . . and it's the best thing I've seen in over a month. There's a fresh bruise on his right cheek. I knew he was in Nashville for a fight, but that evidence makes me pause for a second.

But he's here, and that's all I need right now.

My chest expands and deflates with a much-needed breath as I try to control my emotions. Part of me wants to cry while the other part wants to laugh. It's an odd combination and I don't really know what to do with it. Thankfully, Gunnar saves me from myself. "Hi, Frankie."

His words hit me like a ton of bricks and I sag against the door, letting it hold up my weary body.

I didn't know how badly I've needed to hear him—and *see* him —until right this second. And now I'm wondering how I've made it so long without him.

"Come inside," I say, standing back and giving him space. When he steps across the threshold, his broad chest brushes my shoulder and I close my eyes and inhale. His familiar scent feels like a balm on my worn emotions. When he leans down and brushes a soft kiss on my cheek, I lean into it.

"I've missed you," he whispers. "So much."

We stand there, barely touching, just breathing each other in for what feels like minutes but is probably more like seconds. When he finally moves past me, into the living room, I shut the door and press my back against it. "Thanks for coming over."

He huffs out a laugh, brushing his hand through his hair. It's exactly how I like it—loose, gorgeous, and so Gunnar. It's the version of himself that I feel belongs to me. "I've been waiting on that text for a month. If I hadn't been in Nashville, I would've come sooner."

I give him a small smile, wincing a bit at the hint of pain in his tone. "I'm sorry for not texting you back sooner," I start, pushing off the door. "I just wasn't ready . . ."

"Don't apologize," he says, taking a step toward me before stopping short, and I hate that there's an imaginary barrier between us. The familiarity we'd adapted to so quickly is gone. Gunnar no longer feels like he can reach out and touch me—brush my arm, tuck a piece of hair behind my ear, pull me into a hug, place a kiss on my forehead—without permission.

I did that.

And there's only one way to undo it.

"Want to sit down?" I ask, knowing I'll need the support of my couch to get through this. No way can I stand here and bare my soul without wavering. "I can make us some coffee or tea . . ."

I want to offer a shot of vodka, but that might not be a good idea. Liquor makes me emotional and I don't need any help in that area at the moment.

"Coffee sounds good," Gunnar says, rubbing his palms together like he needs something to do. I can only imagine how hard it is for him to get rid of all the extra adrenaline after a fight. "Want me to help?"

"Sure." Normally, I'd say no, never feeling like I needed or wanted help, but not right now. I want Gunnar's help. I want him close.

After walking into the kitchen, Gunnar fills the coffee pot with water while I scoop the coffee. We work in tandem and it feels natural. Again, the feeling that trumps everything else is relief. That connection I felt hasn't waned; if anything it's strengthened, and I'm grateful.

Maybe we have a chance after all.

Maybe I have a chance.

Leaning against the counter, I face Gunnar and go for something easy to break the ice. "Have you been to Daisy's lately?"

He gives me a side smile, shaking his head. "No."

My stomach drops at that. "Is it because of me? Were you—"

"Cage made me cut out carbs," he says, cutting me off. "And, I didn't feel right going without you."

Peering up at him through my lashes, I watch him for a moment, taking him in. Those eyes, and that face . . . that perfectly imperfect face—and he lets me, doing the same in return.

It doesn't feel uncomfortable or weird, and after a minute or so, I realize we're basically doing one of Samantha's homework tasks without even planning it, which makes me laugh.

"What's so funny?" he asks, crossing his arms over his chest, making his muscles flex on their own accord.

Shaking my head, I think about deflecting, of avoiding, but then I catch myself. "I've been going to therapy," I blurt out, biting down on the corner of my lip. When he doesn't respond to that and just continues to watch me, hanging on my every word and movement, I continue. "Samantha, my therapist, gave me some homework. Most of it sounded awkward and uncomfortable, but this," I motion between us, "it's kind of part of it."

"Standing across from each other?" He cocks his head in curiosity.

Nodding, I add, "And staring at each other for three minutes."

"Oh," Gunnar kicks off the counter, like he's preparing for an athletic feat. "We can totally do this."

His competitiveness comes shining through. I have to guess that's what has kept him coming back every time I've pushed him away. I'm sure there's more to it . . . I hope it's more than him refusing to lose, but that has definitely helped him be so persistent.

Walking over to the microwave, he sets the timer. "Let's do this."

"You don't have to," I tell him, even though I secretly want to. I still think it's kind of weird, but I want to know that we can do the simple things, so hopefully, we can build on them.

"I want to," he says, shaking his head like I'm crazy. "Staring at you is my favorite pastime. It's not a hardship. Let's do this," he repeats, positioning himself across from me, one hand on the start button. "Ready?"

Nodding, I uncross my arms and settle against the cabinet. "Ready."

There's a beep and then Gunnar's eyes are on mine and we stand there, holding each other's gaze. During the first half a minute or so, I fight the urge to look away, feeling the weight of his scrutiny. But then, I settle into it and it goes from feeling like a weight to a warm, comforting embrace.

And now I want a hug. But not just any hug—I want his.

Gunnar's eyes flick briefly to my lips but immediately back to my eyes and I wonder if he's thinking about kissing me, because that's what I think of when I look in his eyes.

At some point, time stands still and we share silent conversation.

I'm glad you're here.

Thank you for texting me.

I missed you.

When the timer goes off, we don't stop staring, but Gunnar eventually smiles. "That wasn't so hard, was it?"

Shaking my head, I reply, "No, not hard at all."

"What other homework has she given you?" he asks, sounding eager to mark everything off the list in one fell swoop. I bet he's always been an overachiever.

"How about we talk first?"

His expression falls a little, probably feeling the same uncertainty and dread I am, but we both know this is how it has to happen. A relationship can't be built on half-truths and avoidance. My mother can attest to that. And that's not how I choose to live my life, not anymore.

I pour two cups of coffee, leaving one black for me and adding two scoops of cream and one scoop of sugar for Gunnar. Like him, I've paid attention. When I hand it to him, he immediately takes a tentative sip, smiling his approval.

"Here, or in there?" I ask, giving him the option of where we sit.

I know how important it is now to have at least a small amount of control in uncertain situations.

"Couch?"

"Okay."

He leads the way and we both take opposite sides, putting a little distance between us, which is good. I need it if I'm going to get through all of this.

Clearing my throat, I glance down at the cup of coffee in my lap and realize this is similar to when my mother and I had our talk. Except now, I'm the one delivering the bad stuff. The sick feeling in the pit of my stomach makes me wince.

"Frankie?" Gunnar asks, drawing my attention back up to him. "Are you okay? If you don't—"

"No," I say, cutting him off. No to whatever he was going to say, whatever out he was getting ready to give me. I don't need it. What I need is to get this out in the open so it can be behind us, instead of between us. "I need to do this. I want to."

After I take a sip of my coffee and use the heat to clear my head a little, I start.

"First, I think you should know that my nightmares are real," I say, figuring this is the best way to start. Since Gunnar was there for a couple of them, it's the easiest way to lay the groundwork for what's to come. "My father was Razor Dennings. You probably don't know of him, but he's currently on death row for twenty-four counts of murder."

When I glance up at Gunnar, his jaw is clenched, but he's doing his best to maintain a neutral expression. I can see the restraint in his eyes.

"When my mom got pregnant with me, she thought we'd be a family, but she was wrong."

I continue telling Gunnar about Razor and my mother and every horrible, sordid detail, leaving nothing out. He deserves to know, and quite frankly, it actually feels good to air it out to someone who isn't my mother or my therapist. It feels like I'm sharing the burden, and if anyone can carry that weight, it's Gunnar.

"He cut me," I finally say, getting to the part that's the hardest to digest. "Not just me, he cut all of his children. By the time my mother was sober enough to do anything about it, I had these." Lifting my shirt, I point out the scars he's already seen. "Thankfully, I don't remember it. I don't want to. My therapist told me there are ways to regain repressed memories, but I choose not to. It's not out of avoidance, but because I don't feel like it would help me at this point in my life."

Gunnar shifts and I meet his eyes. They look as pained as I feel. Telling him takes some of the weight off my chest, but I hate that I'm now burdening him with this truth. But if there's a chance of us having a future, he needs to know about my past.

The strangest sensation washes over me, and I find myself reaching across the couch. Wanting to take away his pain or maybe share my own, I stretch my hand out to him and he greedily accepts. "I'm so sorry, Frankie, for all of it. If I could take it all away, I would."

"The part I started remembering at the end, about my mother . . . that was all real, too. He beat her, and it wasn't until the night of the fight that I really started to see more of those memories. I wish they would've stayed repressed too."

But do I?

If they had, would I know the truth now?

Maybe not.

"What can I do to make it better?" he asks, squeezing my hand. "Tell me—anything, whatever you need. I'll do it."

"You're doing it," I assure him. "Just being here, being you. This is what I need."

We sit there for a few more moments, letting it all sink in, and Gunnar continues to hold my hand, stroking his thumb against my skin. "Don't you have to leave for work in a few hours?" he finally asks.

"Yeah." Glancing at the clock, I see it's been almost an hour since Gunnar got here. My chest feels lighter and my mind clearer than it's been in a long time. "I have to leave by seven thirty."

"You should try to get a couple hours of sleep," he says, his voice barely above a whisper—so gentle, so caring. "I'll go and come back—"

"Stay." It's not really a request, more of a demand, and it takes me back to the first night we spent together. I'm just as desperate for his touch, but for entirely different reasons. That night, I'd needed his strength and comfort.

Tonight, I just need him.

As we lie in bed, Gunnar's arms wrapped around me, I quietly tell him about everything else he's missed in the last month—bits and pieces of therapy, Lisa and Allie showing back up, the improvements to the shelter funded by the money raised from the benefit.

Eventually, we both doze off, and I don't have a nightmare, only dreams of sea-glass eyes.

CHAPTER 27

GUNNAR

*V*ince is giving me a nice workout today. He even gets in a few uppercuts, but I blame the beautiful distraction in the corner of the room.

As part of Frankie's therapy, she started coming to the studio a couple days a week as part of an immersion exercise Samantha wanted her to try. When I chance a glance her way, she touches her pointer finger to her nose, giving me a small smile.

That's our sign, the one that tells me she's fine.

When she started coming here, I needed a way to know she wasn't suffering in silence. So, we came up with something easy and discreet. If she pulls on her ear, that means she needs a break. It's only happened once. Her first time here, she got overwhelmed and we bailed. Instead of sparring with Vince that day, I took Frankie across the street for one of Tempest's muffins.

As long as Frankie's happy, I'm happy.

Of course, I want her to eventually get past her aversion to the sport I love, but I love her more. Even if she never makes it to another one of my fights, I'll be okay with that.

Is it crazy that a cage fighter falls for a nurse with an aversion to violence? Probably.

But that's us, and I love us.

We're both more than the things that define us. Frankie understands I'm not the sport and even though I inflict pain, I don't have ill will toward anyone. I understand that just because she doesn't come to my fights doesn't mean she doesn't support me.

It's unconventional, but it works.

"Keep your hands up," Cage yells, sounding like a mad man. We have another fight next week in Memphis and even though I've won my last two, he's not letting up on the training. If anything, he's working me harder than ever. "Use the decoy!"

As the sweat pours, I give it all I've got.

Left hook, right upper, left hook . . . body shot. Right hook . . . body shot. Left hook . . . right . . .

"Switch it up!"

Jab, cross, left hook, high kick.

Vince grunts, letting me know I hit my mark. When Cage calls for us to take a break, we take off our headgear and gloves, tossing them to the floor as Vince lets out a breathless laugh.

"Fuck," he says, shaking his head. "I feel like you've got a chip on your shoulder tonight."

Cage walks up, handing us two water bottles. "Nah, he's just trying to impress his girl." He shoots Frankie a wink and she blushes a little, shaking her head. The fact that she's still here, even through all of that, makes me happy.

Just sharing this with her feels huge.

"We still on for Genie's later?" Vince asks, scrubbing his sweaty head with a towel. "Frankie? You in?"

She looks up at me, then back to Vince. I see the slight hesitance, but it's like she gives herself a mental pep talk and finally answers, "Sounds fun."

The Frankie I met all those months ago wouldn't even be sitting here. It's Friday night and when I met her, she volunteered on Fridays—which she still does—but then she went home alone, never breaking her routine. Now, she comes here with me on Wednesdays and Fridays after she gets home from the shelter. And she says yes to invites to Genie's.

We still grocery shop together on Tuesday nights, because we want to. It really is the best time to shop the Piggly Wiggly. That's the day they get their weekly shipments in and the produce is the freshest.

Yeah, I keep up with the produce at the Piggly Wiggly.

I also know that tomorrow, when we go to the farmer's market, I'm hitting up Mr. Henson's booth first. Those blueberries go fast. After that, I'm stopping by for Louise Alberti's fried pies. Then, I'll go back to Frankie's booth and keep her company while sneaking in my carbs for the week.

The small town life suits me. Frankie suits me. Actually, she does more than that—she firms up my foundation, giving me something to hold onto that's more permanent than a career or a sport. No matter what happens, as long as I have her, I'll be okay. I'll be better than okay; I'll be the luckiest man in the world.

"I'm going to head home to shower," Vince calls out. "Meet y'all at Genie's in an hour?"

"We'll be there," I tell him, picking up my gloves and hanging them on the hook by the mirrors. "I'm heading up to shower. You staying down here, or you wanna come up?"

Frankie pushes herself up, walking over to me. "When are you going to move in with me?"

I smirk, pulling her hips forward until she's flush with my body. I wiped down with a towel, so I shouldn't get her too sweaty, at least not right now. "I told you," I say, leaning forward and brushing my lips against hers. "We've gotta go on at least twelve dates, and trips to the Piggly Wiggly and Saturdays at the farmer's market don't count."

"That's not fair," she argues, jutting her chin out. I love this side of Frankie—stubborn, bullheaded, and sexy as hell. "You know I work Saturday through Tuesday, volunteer on Wednesdays and Fridays and then come here. It's hard squeezing in *real* dates. And you don't make it any easier with your schedule and trips."

Breathing her in, I pull her hips even closer, wishing we were alone and not in a public place. But fuck if I don't owe Cage months of this shit. The way he and Tempest go at it all the time, I'll never be able to get full retribution. But I don't mind trying.

When my hands travel to her ass, she wiggles out of my embrace, only making things . . . *harder*.

"I'll make you a deal," I tell her, trapping her with my arms, nuzzling my nose in her neck and eliciting a giggle from her.

"What?" she asks, pressing her hands to my chest. Instead of pushing me away, she grabs two fistfuls of my t-shirt, holding me close.

I kiss her neck and feel her body shiver beneath my touch. "Dance with me tonight at Genie's, and we'll count this as two."

"Which makes twelve." She grows still, her hands still holding onto my shirt.

What she doesn't know is I'd started packing my shit two weeks ago and had every intention of moving in with her over the weekend Sweetening the deal with a dance at Genie's tonight was a last-minute game call that totally panned out for me. "I'll move in tomorrow after the farmer's market."

When Frankie read my roommate available ad in the paper, she called me immediately asking me why I was looking for a roommate. She'd almost sounded hurt. I didn't think she'd be ready to make a huge step like that, but I was wrong.

She wanted me to move in that day, but I didn't want to move too fast. Frankie and I have had plenty of setbacks and we're in a good place right now. I didn't want to mess it up. But I'm ready, and if she's ready, then I don't see any reason to wait. I want to see her every morning when we wake up. When she comes home late at night, I want to be there waiting for her.

"How do you feel about adding daily orgasms to your schedule?" I ask, smirking as she fights back a smile. When she shoves lightly at my chest, I begin walking backward into the bathroom, arms raised in surrender as my eyes devour her. I want her today, tomorrow, and every day after that. Moving in with her is the next natural step.

"I can do that," she whispers.

That's what I thought.

After I shower and dress, Frankie and I head out, meeting Vince, Cage, Tempest, and Vali at Genie's. Vince picked out a booth in the back and already had ordered a round of beers before we got there.

Tempest and Frankie slide in next to each other, sharing a quiet hello and a few words I can't hear, but I don't need to. I like the friendship the two of them have started to form. Tempest is a great friend for Frankie, but more than that, I'm so happy that someone else gets to appreciate how great Frankie is.

When a slow song comes on, I slide out of the booth, grabbing Frankie's hand and pulling her out on the dance floor with me.

"I'm not good," she says, giving my hand a little tension.

Turning to face her, I continue to walk backward, still pulling her with me. "You're perfect."

"You know what I mean."

"Just follow my lead," I tell her, wrapping one arm around her waist and bringing our joined hands up to my chest. "I won't let you fall."

She tilts her chin up, those intense eyes boring into mine. "I know."

"Ever danced at a bar before?" I ask, loving every first I'm able to claim of Frankie's.

"No," she says, turning her cheek to my chest and resting it there. "I've never even danced with anyone."

"Not even in high school?"

She lifts her head, giving me a look. "Not even in high school."

I hold her even tighter, hoping to fill up any cracks or lingering hurts, anything to make Frankie a better version of herself. As much as I want to erase her past, I realize it's what made her who she is today, and I love that person—scars and all.

EPILOGUE

FRANKIE

I've always known Tennessee is a beautiful state, but I'm finally realizing just how amazing it really is. The multiple shades of green in the trees, the bright blue sky, and, my favorite—the wildflowers—come together to create the most incredible scenery. I hate feeling like I've taken it for granted all these years.

Now that I've fought the demons of my past and survived, it's as though the fog I didn't realize I was living in has faded away, leaving brightness and clarity in its wake. I smell things differently now and my food tastes better, like all my senses are turned up to one hundred percent.

And then there's my sense of touch.

Everything I come into contact with is intense, especially when it comes to Gunnar. Hugs, caresses, tickles, kisses . . . everything is overwhelming, but only in the best of ways. I swear, I feel like a walking orgasm half the time.

Even though I wasn't near-death a few months ago, I feel like I've been given a new lease on life. It's as if I'm finally living my life, and I owe a lot of that to Gunnar. I'd like to think I would've eventually learned of my past and sought help even if I wasn't with him, but it wouldn't have been as satisfying. Being in therapy and doing the homework I'm given is much easier to get through with his support.

Just like now, as we drive to my mother's home.

Unlike a few months ago, I don't look in the rearview once. The Iron Wraiths are no longer a worry. Outside of the night Crow found me and told me about Razor, they've held up their end of the bargain and kept their distance. When I told Gunnar the entire story, he wanted to track them down and make them pay for stringing me along for the past couple of years. But I wouldn't let him. I refuse to let Razor Dennings mess up anyone else's life, especially Gunnar's.

He has too much going for him. Now that I know all there is to know about mixed martial arts and the UFC, I know he could get in big trouble for fighting outside the ring. I also know he'd risk something like that for me, but I don't need him to fight my battles.

Besides, Razor is behind bars for life.

One of these days, I might dig a little deeper into who he was and explore the possibility of finding my siblings. But for now, I'm happy with my life and the family I have.

About a month after my mother shed light on my hidden memories, I made the decision to forgive her. We talked, we cried, and then we decided to move on—together. We both know she hasn't always been an ideal mother, but I understand she did the best she could, given the circumstances, and that's good enough for me. I can't change the past, but it's up to me how I live the rest of my life.

Our relationship never has been and never will be perfect, but I decided I'd much rather have her in my life than not.

Things are still strained at times and I wish my mom would speak with Samantha or find a therapist of her own, but that needs to be her decision. She's slowly coming out of her shell, though, and she's starting to branch out more with what she creates and sells at the farmer's market, which is why we're here.

"Come in." She greets us from her porch with a smile, motioning for us to hurry inside. "You have to try my new jams."

Gunnar and I hide our grimaces from her, but not from each

other. We've both tasted some not-so-great concoctions over the last few weeks, so we're not very eager to try anything else. But we do, of course.

As soon as we step inside the kitchen, my mother shoves two spoons at us with a healthy scoop of jam in them.

I tentatively taste, offering myself up as a guinea pig to save Gunnar from unnecessary harm, and am pleasantly surprised with the flavor, so I finish off what's left on the spoon. Gunnar follows suit and gives a nod of approval. The raspberry flavor is delicious, but there's something else I can't put a name to. "Wow, Mom, that's really good. It's different and has a nice kick to it. What did you add to it? Jalapenos?"

"No, Moscato!" she answers, clearly proud of herself.

"You made boozy jam?" Gunnar asks, cackling. "That's awesome, Miss C." I'm dumbstruck as I watch him high-five my mother. Not only has he swept me off my feet and made me want things I'd never dreamed possible, but he's breaking down my mom's walls too.

"Do you think they'll sell? I really think they'd be a hit with the local ladies who brunch. Maybe I can go with you next week and help sell them, depending on how this week's market goes."

I'm obviously not the only one who's been changing for the better around here.

"That'd be great, Mom," I say, encouragingly. She's suggested joining us a few times lately but it hasn't happened yet. I'm just thrilled she's even considering it, and I'm hopeful that one day she'll follow through.

Gunnar takes my hand and gives it a little squeeze. "Want to take a walk with me before we load up?"

"Sure." I smile at him, wondering what he's up to. "Mom, we're gonna go for a walk but we won't be gone too long."

"That's fine, dear. Have fun." Paying us no mind, except for the small, content smile on her face, she goes about ladling her new creation into jars.

Gunnar takes my hand again, interlocking our fingers, as we

begin our walk. My mother's property is quite large and the grass needs to be cleared soon, but it's also very peaceful. I haven't mentioned anything to Gunnar, but I could see us building our own home out here one of these days.

We walk in silence for a few minutes before stopping at my favorite spot. It has a few large trees that provide a wonderful shade to sit in while looking out at the nearby pond.

"I love it here," I say for no real reason.

"I know you do. That's why this is the perfect place."

"The perfect place for what?"

"The perfect place to fall." He gives me my favorite smile of his, the one that makes his eyes sparkle the most. It's also the one he gives only to me.

"I hate to break it to you, Beefcake, but I've already fallen for you." I slip my arms around him and pull our bodies together.

"Frankie, I want you to do the Trust Fall with me."

"What? Why?" The Trust Fall is the only homework assignment from Samantha I haven't completed. Not because I don't want to, but because I think it's silly at this point. I know I can trust Gunnar, and I do. I trust him with my whole heart, so why he thinks we need to do this is beyond me.

"It's important to me, and it should be to you, too. It's the last step and you refuse to do it because you think it's silly. I've done research of my own, you know, and it has its merits. I mean, why not do it? It could be fun. You never know."

His eyes catch on my collarbone and I automatically know what he's looking at. A scar. I used to be ashamed of them, afraid of what they could represent. Being with Gunnar, though, has helped me embrace them rather than hide them. They're a part of me. They help make me who I am, and I like who I am.

I watch Gunnar lick his lips before leaning over and placing a gentle kiss on top of the puckered flesh. Every time he sees a scar he kisses it. Or touches it, almost reverently. He wants them to represent only good things, he's told me before, and what's better than his kisses? I can only think of one thing and if he keeps putting his mouth on my skin like he's doing right now, I'm going to make him take me right here, right now.

"Gunnar," I whisper.

"Fall for me. I want to catch you."

It's in this moment I realize he wants to do the test, not just for me, but for him, as well. He wants it for us and I can't find it in me to deny him. "Okay."

There's that smile again.

"Okay, turn around and take a couple of steps forward. I'm right behind you. Whenever you're ready, I'm right here," he assures me.

I might trust Gunnar with all my heart but that doesn't keep me from worrying about the fall. It's not that I think he won't catch me, it's more about me worrying that I'll fall and hurt myself. Or him. I don't want to embarrass myself in front of Gunnar. I know it sounds silly and juvenile, but it's how I feel.

"Come on, baby. You can do it."

"Alright," I hesitate for a few more seconds, taking a deep breath. When I let it out slowly, I push out every negative thought with it.

I can do this.

I can do this for me.

I can do this for us.

Closing my eyes, I focus on the sun warming my skin, the water splashing in the nearby pond, and the birds chirping in the trees. With fear far from my mind, I'm completely at peace.

So, I fall.

Being caught by Gunnar Erickson is the best feeling in the world —exhilarating, scary, safe, warm, and a lot like something I want to do forever.

ACKNOWLEDGMENTS

A common theme in our books is family and that's because we value ours immensely. Sometimes, it's the family you're born into and other times, it's the one you make for yourself. We consider ourselves lucky to have both. To our children, who are more like adults these days, thank you for being understanding when we're locked away in the writing cave for days and weeks. Sometimes it feels like our houses are going to grow legs and run away from us. So, thanks for holding down the fort and living off ramen and pizza.

We have an amazing support group.

Pamela Stephenson is always there from the beginning, watching and reading as the story takes shape. Her cheerleading skills are second to none. Thanks for being you, Pamela!!

We'd also like to thank Nikki, our editor. Thank you for always approaching each new story with an insightful eye. You teach us things along the way, and we'd like to think we're better writers because of you. Here's to a dozen more books!

For these Smartypants Romance (SPR) books we've found a couple new people to add to our arsenal of amazingness. Heather, our alpha reader. Thank you for your wonderfully insightful feedback.

Janice, you're a proofreading wizard! Thank you for polishing our manuscript and making it shine.

To Penny Reid, the evil overlord and creator of the Green Valley universe. Thank you, from the bottom of our hearts. We're so grateful for this chance to step into your world and get creative with your characters. Thank you for trusting us and believing in us.

And to all the other SPR authors, we love each and every one of you, and we're so happy and blessed to be a part of such a wonderful group of women. You're all badass boss babes and you inspire us every single day!

Thank you to all our new readers we've found on this SPR journey. If you're not a part of our Jiffy Kate's Southern Belles reader group on Facebook, we'd love to have you! All of you make our days better.

It takes a village and we're so happy you're a part of ours.

Much love,

Jiffy Kate

ABOUT THE AUTHOR

Jiffy Kate is the joint pen name for Jiff Simpson and Jenny Kate Altman. They're co-writing besties who share a brain. They also share a love of cute boys, stiff drinks, and fun times.

Together, they've written over twenty stories. Their first published book, Finding Focus, was released in November 2015. Since then, they've continued to write what they know--southern settings full of swoony heroes and strong heroines.

* * *

Website: http://www.jiffykate.com
Facebook: https://www.facebook.com/jiffykate
Goodreads: https://www.goodreads.com/author/show/
7352135.Jiffy_Kate
Twitter: @jiffykatewrites
Instagram: @jiffykatewrites

Find Smartypants Romance online:
Website: www.smartypantsromance.com
Facebook: www.facebook.com/smartypantsromance/
Goodreads: www.goodreads.com/smartypantsromance
Twitter: @smartypantsrom
Instagram: @smartypantsromance

OTHER BOOKS BY JIFFY KATE

Finding Focus Series:

Finding Focus

Chasing Castles

Fighting Fire

Taming Trouble

French Quarter Collection:

Turn of Fate

Blue Bayou

Come Again

Neutral Grounds

Good Times (coming summer 2020)

Table 10 Novella Series:

Table 10 part 1

Table 10 part 2

Table 10 part 3

New Orleans Revelers:

The Rookie and The Rockstar

TVATV (coming fall 2020)

Smartypants Romance:

Stud Muffin (Fighting for Love, book 1)

Beef Cake (Fighting for Love, book 2)

Eye Candy (Fighting for Love, book 3)

Standalones:

Watch and See

No Strings Attached

OTHER BOOKS BY SMARTYPANTS ROMANCE

Park Ranger Series

Happy Trail by Daisy Prescott (#1)

Stranger Ranger by Daisy Prescott (#2)

The Leffersbee Series

Been There Done That by Hope Ellis (#1)

The Higher Learning Series

Upsy Daisy by Chelsie Edwards

Seduction in the City

Cipher Security Series

Code of Conduct by April White (#1)

Code of Honor by April White (#2)

Cipher Office Series

Weight Expectations by M.E. Carter (#1)

Sticking to the Script by Stella Weaver (#2)

Cutie and the Beast by M.E. Carter (#3)

Made in the USA
Coppell, TX
12 May 2023

16713831R00146